'THE FIFTY-FI[illegible] IT!'

Just before Montgomery's [illegible]al attack at Alamein, an Australian infantry battalion was ordered into an action which would have ordinarily been given to a brigade.

'The Fifty-Fifth can do it,' the General said.

This powerful novel tells the story of the doomed Fifty-Fifth. It is a startling and unforgettably true-to-life story of men at war.

Also by Eric Lambert

THE TWENTY THOUSAND THIEVES
THE VETERANS
WATERMEN
THE DARK BACKWARD
THE REHABILITATED MAN
BALLARAT
THE DRIP-DRY MAN
KELLY
HIROSHIMA REEF
THE LONG WHITE NIGHT
A SHORT WALK TO THE STARS

and published by Corgi editions

Eric Lambert

Glory Thrown In

CORGI BOOKS
A DIVISION OF TRANSWORLD PUBLISHERS LTD

GLORY THROWN IN

A CORGI BOOK 0 552 10192 3

Originally published in Great Britain by
Frederick Muller Ltd.

PRINTING HISTORY
Frederick Muller edition published 1959
Corgi edition published 1961
Corgi edition re-issued 1963
Corgi edition re-issued 1976

Copyright © 1959 Eric Lambert

Conditions of sale
1: This book is sold subject to the condition that it shall not, by way of trade *or otherwise*, be lent, re-sold, hired out or otherwise *circulated* without the publisher's prior consent in any form of binding or cover other than that in which it is published *and without a similar condition including this condition being imposed on the subsequent purchaser*.
2: This book is sold subject to the Standard Conditions of Sale of Net Books and may not be re-sold in the U.K. below the net price fixed by the publishers for the book.

This book is set in 9 pt. Times.

Corgi Books are published by Transworld Publishers Ltd.,
Century House, 61–63 Uxbridge Road,
Ealing, London, W.5.
Made and printed in Great Britain by
Hunt Barnard Printing Ltd., Aylesbury, Bucks.

594-78

'Got glory thrown in
As it were with every ton'

C. Day Lewis

INFORMATION

1

From the sky, the flier saw the desert as a stretch of paint-work executed by an ochre-ish brush. A second artist who went under the name of Man had scored, scattered, and traced his own devices across it. Vehicle tracks were endless threads of black cotton; strong-posts and trench systems strange black geometrical designs painted by some surrealist who was not quite certain what he was about. The tracks ended seemingly in nothing, but the sharp shadow of the camouflaged gun or tank sometimes gave it away.

For the shadows followed the sun, burning whitely and cloudily from the perfect sky. Perfect day after day, and the moon perfect by night.

Northward of the desert area called after the nearest railway station, El Alamein, the sea. Burning bluely back at the sky with a shirred and polished surface, except near the shore where the beaches tore it into white fringes, and the water was one green, then another, then finally gold.

Scenically, the flier had the best of it.

• • • • •

The infantryman saw it from a slit in the ground. The desert for him had no appearance of paintwork. He lived in it, wormed into it for refuge; it encompassed him, he breathed it in. "Picturesque" would have been his very last adjective, had he bothered to think of another than "bloody". To the flier the desert looked always the same, but the infantryman saw it changed hourly: by the wind which whipped up its powdered surface into prickling yellow mists that fled across it as if maddened by the *khamsin*; by fleeing vehicles which created lazier, thicker mists; by blossoming explosions making dirty clouds, which sometimes dissipated to unveil the prone or writhing form.

Beneath the camouflage nets and the roofs of dug-outs ("doovers" the Australians called them) the industry of war proceeded. Gun positions were adjusted, observation posts set up, forward posts dug by night and stealthily manned. And all the time there was thought, intense, charted, organised—either side of the ridges which divided, as if in the name of merciful fates, the German and the British armies. The ridges where the sunlight striking and rebounding on the stones looked from the air like great, restless waves.

• • • • •

The Germans had thought that Egypt was theirs. All that stood in their way was the exhausted Eighth Army huddled in the gap between the Qattara Depression and the Mediterranean. Mussolini had flown over to Tobruk, with a fine brass band, ready for the triumphal entry into Cairo. Trucks waited just behind the front lines, loaded with paper flags for the liberated populace to wave. Confident members of the Afrika Corps had not bothered to dig themselves in as they rested overnight before the march of victory on the cities. Thus they were found by the Ninth Australian Division as it swept into the gap one night, slaughtered the unprepared Germans, re-took the ground known as Tel El Aisa or the Hill of Jesus, holding it against the tanks and infantry that came at them next day and for several days thereafter, until the Germans realised that the plum of Egypt was not yet theirs. Several weeks of almost daily engagements passed before the Germans went back behind the ridges, resigned for the time being to static warfare, wobbling a little uncertainly at the end of their long line of communication. The Australian casualties were so huge they meant, virtually, extinction for one or two battalions. One of the most severely mauled was the Fighty Fifty-Fifth—"Numerella's own."

• • • • •

Supposing you were a flier in that perfect sky and you imagined your machine had become a camera lens. Curiosity would draw you earthward, until the paintwork became solidity, and the black geometrical blobs were seen as depths where men sheltered from the enemy's missiles. The shadows would grow beside them the forms of tanks, trucks, and armoured cars; what you had seen from the sky as nothing but a part of the desert's surface is now a net in whose cool shadows beneath there are men.

The whole enormous painting that you saw from the sky, is, in fact, hived with men. Men afraid. Men desperate. Patient. Exhausted. Half mad.

In a corner of the seemingly incoherent pattern lurked the remnants of the Fifty-Fifth.

2

LIEUTENANT-COLONEL VICTOR KIRK, M.C., D.C.M., Commanding Officer of the Fifty-Fifth Australian Infantry Battalion, was thinking about his son. He felt a little annoyed at himself—the signal which had just come through to him, to the effect that Lieutenant Ted Kirk, of the Forty-Second Battalion had been awarded the M.C., had found him mysteriously unmoved. His own boy, too. He ought to be on the blower, declaiming "Good show!" or something. Stainforth his Adjutant was hovering like a bloody night-nurse in the adjoining dug-out, expecting just that.

Suddenly Stainforth was back in the Colonel's dug-out, and the Colonel, looking bleakly up, was impelled to compare Lionel Stainforth with Edward Kirk and come down heavily in favour of Edward Kirk—blood aside.

Stainforth was a good adjutant, and everything the Colonel detested. Along with the Baillies, the Olivers, and the Orfords, the Stainforths were big names in the Numerella district. In peace-time the Colonel could not have hoped for an invitation to dinner from any of them—not that such hopes had ever crossed his mind. The Squatocracy he found unfailingly ridiculous. British snobbery the Colonel understood. It was something bred in the bone. Snobbery founded on nothing but vast acres and too much money was merely vulgar. Watching the graceless scrambles in Numerella for acquaintance with Vice-Royalty, he had often been moved to jeer "There's no snob like an Australian snob."

What did the consequential little bastard want to suggest? Trying to get the Forty-Second on the line, so he could bleat his congratulations to Ted? Putting in one more futile word for Price-Gore?

"What do you want?" asked the Colonel ungraciously. (Didn't even have the guts to answer back "What have you got?")

Stainforth cleared his throat. "New officers, sir."

The Colonel grunted, not without pleasure.

"Nobody's going to OCTU, if that's what you want to know."

"I thought that now might be a good time——"

"I know what you thought. I might send Corporal Price-Gore to OCTU. Well, I need rifle platoon commanders, and I'm commissioning three sergeants in the field."

"I see, sir. Which sergeants, may I ask?"

"Green, Britton, and Rogers."

"Not Home, sir?"

"Doc Home? Definitely not. Whatever for?"

"You did say he was the best sergeant in the Battalion, sir."

"Yes, and he'd make the Battalion's worst officer."

The Colonel rose. "You tell Price-Gore, if he's got ambitions, to transfer to the Pay Corps or Ordnance. He's not getting any rank out of me just because he happened to be your boss."

Before the Adjutant could protest, the Colonel was out in the sun. Far above, a droning reconnaissance plane was no more than the flash of a fish's scale. Battalion Headquarters was well tucked into the desert, transport down in their pits, Vickers guns and six-pounders quiet but deadly below the camouflage netting, patterned with scrappy yellow like the desert. Like some great chameleon, the Battalion absorbed the hues of its surroundings.

There was no gunfire.

The Colonel made towards the pit where his jeep resided. A man whose face, arms, and legs were all but black beside his yellow-white shirt and shorts, rose from the dust almost at the Colonel's feet, tin hat set far back on his head like a halo. It was the Colonel's driver.

"You going anywhere, Boss?"

"Yes. On my own. And put your boots on. Don't you know this dust is full of germs?"

The man shrugged and sank into the dust again. Clearly, the Colonel heard another voice ask from the darkness of the driver's dug-out:

"Was that old Diddly-Dum?"

The Colonel grinned to himself, slid down the ramp to his jeep, and got it into motion, out on to the flat, stony ground. As he passed Headquarters dug-out he yelled to the attendant Stainforth:

"I'll be at Don Company!"

. . . . .

The Private they called Horrible John sat back in the trench and declared:

"I think I'll desert."

He had a great, long, melon-shaped jaw and a three-day beard on it sprouted like hog's bristles.

None of his companions made any comment. Every Other Ranker in the army had at least once in his life uttered such a sentiment. There were four of them in the wide trench, three privates and their sergeant, Alex Home. It was not their own trench, being part of an abandoned mortar pit; but the direction in which it ran put it for the time being in the shade.

Above them, the few sounds there were on the desert were muffled. A plane like a fly against a window, a burst of gunfire like fingers drummed on a table. Down here life was on the very simplest level. Nothing to see but a rectangle of sky and the sour-smelling walls of the trench, and of course the other men. But you didn't notice them, you didn't really observe them any more. They became more real for you when they got killed, and you missed them.

There were a lot of men being missed.

Alone in a neighbouring pit, a very tall and thin man, of about forty years of age, lay at full length trying to write in pencil on a Salvation Army letter pad. This is what he had written:

"As we crouched you and I, to the walls of our ground slit,
 When the guns had found us,
The shrill metal sundering ran in long tongues,
 Sang with affliction all around us—
 You cried at the wrong of it.

Wrong! All wrong! For a moment you lived as a child,
The face in your hands was a child's at injustice—
  All young and wild.
But the driven-thing gloam of your eyes was to me
  All the sadness, madness of humanity."

The author's brilliant blue eyes regarded his work critically. He raised them to the sky and saw instead battle-dust. Agitated figures moved behind the dust like shadows on a blind, sometimes sank into it, and the whole shadow-play shuddered and leapt to the ceaseless impact of bombardment. It was roofed blackly by air-bursts, as though the sun had been eclipsed.

Should it be "gloam" or "gleam"? "Gleam" was sharper, but "gloam" was sadder, it stood out more and made you see the eyes, softened perhaps, because death was already in them.

Yes! That was how Charlie's eyes had appeared. There had been no light in them, only the dull glint of death foreseen. For the hundredth time he saw the vision of the thing that he alone would recall. The Germans, eleven of them rising suddenly over on Don Company's flank, with three Spaudaus, which, if the Germans could get them going, could have wiped Don Company out. He and Charlie alone in the thick, swirling dust.

The stick grenade burst right next to him and as he spun about he lost his tommy-gun. He staggered and groped around in that yellow mist. Charlie's slim young figure loomed for a second beside him, Charlie's voice said: "I'll be with you in a minute." Then Charlie walked straight at the eleven Germans with his gun coughing out short bursts. He became just a blot on the mist, out of which his voice cried weirdly. Then one of the Spandaus fired.

The man reliving the vision saw the figure of Charlie quietly panting its last across the corpse of the last German he had shot. *Oh, yes, Charlie had undoubtedly saved the Company and only he, Christy, saw it. So there was nothing for Charlie in the subsequent handing out of medals.*

Nothing for Charlie Mann, aged twenty-four, best friend of Arnold Christy, late of Numerella.

"Hey, Corpus!" A voice hailed him shrilly from the trench where Doc Home and three others sheltered, and Christy, called Corpus, came unwillingly back to the present.

"Hallo!" he called back.

"Horrible reckons he's gonna desert!"

"Good riddance," said Christy.

. . . . .

The Colonel sent his jeep skidding along the track, dotted with signposts low to the ground so that they cast no shadows for any aerial photographer. On either side the desert was scattered with twenty-five pounder gun-pits, spread with camouflage nets that looked from a distance like *bedouin* tents. Not that the *bedouin* would dream of pitching tents in such a spot. No, it took civilised white men, fighting a war, to think that one up.

Price-Gore! The Colonel ground his teeth silently over the ridiculous name. The men invented awful variations of it, like Vice-Whore, Mice-Gnaw, or Twice-Poor. The Colonel knew the story of Price-Gore backwards, and was tired of it.

There was one type of Englishman coming to Australia who was epitomised in Price-Gore. Lower middle-class. An exaggerated reproduction of his social superiors. For him, Australia was still one of the "colonies", the Australian people a somewhat wild, *gauche* (but loyal to the bone, my word!) offshoot of the parent stem; ready at the first nod to pour forth and die repairing any blunders of Downing Street. Such men either altered, cast off their shell, and lived like Australians, or returned home bewildered, to the sound cruel Australian mirth they would remember to their dying day. Price-Gore had been unusually lucky. The big squatters of the Numerella district, busy erecting their own aristocracy—hence Squattocracy—had found Price-Gore at the right time. The British oil company for which he worked had built a depot for Central Queensland at Numerella, and, true to its policy of keeping all its top men English, had made Price-Gore General Manager. To be in charge of that sprawling depot beside the railway, with its huge tanks interfering with the skyline, its own siding, made Price-Gore somebody in Numerella.

Price-Gore read the mood of Numerella's upper strata accurately and played up to it—for which the Colonel did not blame him in the least. The Colonel knew, for instance, that the man's real name was Edwin Price Gore, the Price being merely a middle name, the hyphen appearing later when Gore took up the role of Numerella's Resident Englishman.

The English public school, whose blazer Price-Gore flaunted luridly on the cricket field before going in to play a wholly perpendicular bat, was not even listed among the minor public schools. This much the Colonel knew from his relations in Scotland.

Stainforth, youngest of four sons and crowded out by his brothers as far as the running of their property went, had turned to business and become Price-Gore's Supervisor.

Price-Gore must have been badly disappointed in Stainforth. Some of Numerella's upper fifty had come into the Fifty-Fifth as officers, others as privates with their commissions just over the next hill. Price-Gore had joined the Battalion two days before it sailed, as a private, and the commission had not eventuated. In the first place Colonel Oliver had got himself taken prisoner at Tobruk and Kirk had been appointed C.O. The General wanted soldiers now. As Kirk's Company Commander at Gallipoli, he had seen Sergeant Kirk lead his platoon to the top of the ridge in the face of the enemy guns, killing thirty-odd Turks on the way up. So it was Kirk and the Fifty-Fifth—and the General was happy. You could rely on the Numerella mob.

And the Colonel wanted platoon commanders, not good executives like Price-Gore. If Stainforth was killed then Price-Gore would make a first-class Adjutant. As a platoon commander he would be hopeless. The thought of the twittering Price-Gore trying to gain some sort of authority over men like Doc Home, Horrible John Jones, or Corpus Christy was too much for the Colonel's funny-bone.

So Price-Gore stayed an orderly room corporal and Stainforth might be looking for a new job when it was all over.

"Old Diddly-Dum," indeed!

. . . . .

"Why shouldn't I desert?" asked Horrible John. "You've got morals, you blokes, but I haven't."

"You're a cert for the Senate some day," observed Christy, who had joined them in the shade of the old trench.

Doc Home leaned hungrily towards him, his long slits of eyes like wings in his pointed face. In profile, his nose was a perfect arc. Christy often described his expression as that of a *bedouin* anticipating loot.

"Corpus," he asked, "why don't you go into politics? You're a rebel."

"Politics is no place for a rebel," retorted Christy. "Politics are for conformists, and crooks, and time-servers."

"He's off!" announced Horrible John.

Christy disregarded him and continued. He was talking for his own benefit mostly.

"As soon as a cause becomes organised it becomes corrupted. As soon as it becomes successful it becomes intolerable. Revolutions devour their best children."

"That poetry?" asked Horrible John.

"No. History."

"Is that why you're always magging with Pascoe?" Horrible John went on. "Wasn't he a history writer?"

"He's an historian, yes."

When Horrible John tried to look innocent, he looked witless. This was his appearance at the moment.

"So that's why you and him are always talking. And here's me thinkin' you was crawling for stripes."

Even the two other privates, who were new to Don Company, found amusing the thought of Christy humbling himself for rank.

The conversation had taken a turn which bored Doc. He wanted sensation.

"Tell 'em about yourself," he urged Horrible John, indicating the newcomers.

Jones took up the role that Doc so often thrust on him. The Shocker.

"Well, you see," began Horrible John. "I'm a bastard." His new audience looked unmoved. "I mean me parents weren't married. I'm a real bastard. I never even knew me parents. I was raised," he said proudly, "in a church home. And what a home! I knew the facts of life when you jokers were learning your alphabet. There was this superintendent, you see. A dirty big flabby bloke. We used to call him Mud Guts. He was a perv. Special attention given to small boys. Then there was the Matron, a big horse-faced sheila with a beam like a battleship. Her first name was Irma, but the boys always called her Squirmer. She liked the big boys. There weren't many of the big blokes she didn't break in as far as the actual facts of life were concerned."

"But didn't they ever get found out?"

"Not in my time. You see, the matron and the superintendent had a sort of pact like. Each kept quiet about the other's lurk."

"Here, did either of them have a go at you?"

"Both of them. Me and Mud Guts didn't get on, see. I turned round and kicked his shins when he clouted me. I'd been there a long time before he tried anything with me. I never forget it. I went straight through the window of his study yelling 'Poofter!' at him as I went. I ran straight to Matron to tell her what had happened to me."

"Gawd!" exclaimed one of the new men. "What a lovely place."

"The best is yet to come," Horrible John assured him. "After I finish telling old Squirmer all about it, she says oh dear me, we can't have that, can we? Big boys aren't meant for that sort of thing. So then she starts to show me what big boys *are* meant for."

"You mean she——"

"I mean she took off her big pink bloomers in the middle of her room."

"And how old were you?"

"Me? About fourteen."

"Gawd stiffen the wombats!"

"We used to compare notes about her in the dormitory at night," Horrible John concluded.

"Dirty old bitch!"

"Oh, yair?" said Horrible John. "Well, let me tell you something, mug. Squirmer had a heart of gold. None of us was any the worse off because of her. She had a heart of gold as long as she got her oats."

"These big sexy sorts are often like that."

"Best friend I ever had," asserted Horrible John.

"A sort of matriarch," murmured Christy.

"Don't you go calling her names either," snarled Horrible John.

• • • • •

The Colonel had stopped his jeep to watch a Stuka "parade" some miles over to the south. Like great black birds, even in formation the Stukas had a poised look. One by one they began to peel off and their engines changed to a screaming tone. They seemed to hurtle earthwards as if to dash themselves to pieces on the desert, only to pull beautifully from the dive to plane upward like hawks on the wind. Below them, as their bombs hit, the dust leapt up into towering mustard-coloured walls that swirled and boiled like a surf.

About time the Kittyhawks showed up, if they were coming this morning. As if to his summons, a flight of them specked the sky in the east, far above the Stukas. Portly, gross things as fighters went, all at sea against the Messerschmitts, pulling sluggishly out of their dive and far too fat on a turn, but these things made them ideal against the Stukas. Just the right edge on the Stukas but not too much of an edge. Sheer hell to handle, an air liaison officer had told him; only the Australians were mad enough to fly these new American fighters with a landing speed of a hundred and twenty.

The Kittyhawks were in their dive now. The Stukas held their formation and their dive-drill as though there were no other planes in the sky. The Kitties would sow havoc, but the Stukas not shot out of formation would carry out the mission. Three turned idly into their death spins as he watched. They were too far away to see them hit the earth; there was a boom and an upsurge of black smoke.

The Kitties went far into the sun to bank, then came again as the remaining Stukas dived on. The Australians caught them sometimes in formation, sometimes as they came up tiredly from the dive. The Colonel counted eight Stukas down.

It was all over in fifteen minutes. The Stukas fled for home with the Kitties after them; but the Kitties would not pursue too far, in case there were Messers abroad. The bomb-fog on the horizon was sluggish now; it thinned, and soon was only a haze. The Colonel started the jeep.

The desert was silent again, the sky no longer profaned. His thoughts came back to his son Ted. His M.C. was something he would enjoy writing to Freda about. He imagined her stopping everyone she passed in the main street of Numerella, saying: "My son has won the Military Cross!" There would be nothing untoward in that. It would be almost her duty to tell them; for in Numerella any news about a member of "Numerella's Own" was public property. When a man was decorated, the whole town was proud; when a man was killed all Numerella grieved.

For as long as the war lasted, her position as wife of the colonel of "Numerella's Own" made her the town's first lady—which must at this very moment be putting Orford, Stainforth, Baillie, and Oliver noses badly out of joint. Freda Kirk, wife of a district inspector of the Queensland Railways, on five hundred a year, with a six-roomed weatherboard house, a solitary cow in the back paddock and a '35 model Chev. No polo, no Brisbane at Show Time with Pimms Number One in the lounge at Lennons, no handshakes with the Governor . . . oh, the gall that must be in them!

The Colonel laughed. Freda would handle them. The wives and mothers would be saying what certain of his own officers were saying: what a pity Oliver had gone! There would be a little more gall spread around when they heard he had "bowlered" two of the Baillies—one for cowardice, the other for inadequacy.

Freda would understand all of this. Her blind spot was Ted. That woman's mind of hers could not bring her to see why he, Colonel of the Fifty-Fifth, should not have his own son in the Forty-Second. In response to anxious mothers, he kept an eye on men of tender ages, exhorting them to keep their heads down, write home regularly, and be careful when they went into brothels; but all his anxiety and solicitude for Ted—that had to come from a distance. What did she care if some of these Numerella bags whispered "favouritism"? They should be the last ones to talk of privilege and back-scratching. As for what any of the men in the Fifty-Fifth might say—he was Colonel, wasn't he?

Yes, dear Freda, that was just it. He was Colonel. Under Army Law, a man could claim his younger brother to his own unit; fathers and sons had been known to serve together . . .

But not this father and this son.

• • • • •

"So yer see?" Horrible John was saying in a parody of Christy's manner. "I have no debt to society. Society's me enemy like. I joined the army 'cause I wanted a trip abroad, and I've paid for me trip in two campaigns—Tobruk, and here——"

"This campaign's not over," Doc interrupted. "It's just started."

"I fought on Jesus," said Jones righteously.

"Fought on Jesus!" exclaimed one of the new men in outraged tones.

"Hill of Jesus," Doc explained. "Tel El Aisa. Anyway, it was west of Jesus."

Somewhere west of Jesus, dreamed Christy—a good line . . .

"Murder it was," Horrible John told his audience. "Here, Doc, how many blokes did we lose?"

"Three hundred."

"Numerella's gonna be terrible short of tool after the war," Horrible John went on. "I'm getting out while I'm in one piece so I can go back and take up full time stud duties with the sheilas."

"What a bastard!" Doc told the new men.

Horrible John had one touchy nerve; he loved referring to himself as a bastard, but would tolerate it from nobody else.

"I'll foggin' do you," he promised Doc.

Doc spat. "You couldn't pull the feathers off a sick duck."

. . . . .

Diddly-dum . . . diddly-dum . . . The Colonel had been dreaming as he drove; for a few seconds he had been persuaded his jeep was making just such a noise.

Diddly-dum . . . diddly-dum . . . The eternal refrain of the Queensland trains as they penetrated the gigantic spaces. Through the bald brown hills where the stout grey sheep meandered, or spread in front of the drover a moving carpet, where the dead timber paraded along the skyline like contorted gibbets. Through the still, silent forests of grey-green gum; thence up to the cattle country, Numerella country, through the plains of burning green with the great swamps where the cattle stood and never saw their own feet and ibis, heron, and crane posed like those birds on Chinese screens. The jungles where the flying possum planed down the higher branches, the kangaroo rat sniffled in the undergrowth, the flying-foxes hung like evil fruit, and the budgerigars descended from the sky in strident, brilliant clouds. Through Numerella, where the line ran for a mile parallel with the main street and you admired the lovely alternation of scarlet flowering gum and lucent blue jacaranda, or envied the cattle drovers lounging with beer beneath the languishing branches and little pink pods of the peppercorns.

Diddly-dum . . . diddly-dum . . . On, out into the burning stony plains, the ironstone ridges, the small mountains made by man in his underground pursuit of gold, silver, lead . . . Diddly-dum . . .

So Vic Kirk, a railway district inspector (a district as large as England and Scotland together) had joined the Fifty-Fifth as Captain, Commander of Don Company, whose members boasted men like Christy who had worked with him and loved the spaces they traversed in their work. It was only to be expected that men would murmur diddly-dum from the corners of their mouths as they passed him. It caught on throughout the Battalion. Then that bloody fool of an R.S.M. took notice of it, and every Battalion parade the ranks sounded like the approach of the Bundaberg Express, with DIDDLY-DUM . . . DIDDLY-DUM . . . and the R.S.M. stalking furiously up and down the ranks peering into each face to detect the slightest flicker of a lip; a hopeless task, since you could go *diddly-dum* without moving your lips; the sound following the R.S.M.'s infuriated progress like a malignant tide. DIDDLY-DUM . . . DIDDLY-DUM.

Came the day Don Company mounted Brigade Guard and the R.S.M. drilled them purposely himself. They were exemplary soldiers for the first hour of it—then they decided they had had enough . . . Diddly-dum . . . diddly-dum . . .

"Oh, my God!" moaned the R.S.M. "It's in the guard!"

They spoke of it as though it were some disease.

Well, he had stopped it in Don Company, not that any other officer would have believed him if he had explained how. He had simply called out his company at two o'clock one morning, lined them up in the freezing cold, and asked them as a personal favour, not to do it.

Ted roared when he heard the story.

Ted. All other things being equal, he wouldn't have wanted him in the Forty-Second. One of the Kirks had to survive.

The Colonel lived in a fore-vision. In this vision the Fifty-Fifth was doomed. He had pictured its doom in his dreams in a dozen different ways. In every infantry division, there is one expendable battalion. It is proven, reliable, understood. For that which is most dirty and most desperate, it is, by its very nature, always chosen. The Fifty-Fifth was that battalion.

Here he was at Don Company.

A Numerella man stood up in his pit and called:

"Can I see you for a minute, Boss?"

"What do you want?" growled the Colonel.

"What have you got?"

The man was not to know why the Colonel laughed at such an old retort.

3

"Go and get Sergeant Rogers," ordered the Colonel, and as he waited surveyed what he could see of the Don Company positions. Pascoe as usual had sited them excellently: crossfire from the Brens, Vickers in support with interlocking beaten zones, six-pounders well back to draw the tanks through and keep them shut in—a lesson from the old Tobruk days.

The Fifty-Fifth was well behind in support at the moment, and if any Germans penetrated this far it would mean Rommel had begun his big push to Alex. It wasn't often the Fifty-Fifth was in support.

Sergeant Rogers appeared, a severe-faced, squat, bow-legged man, bitten hard in his country's cause. A very good soldier.

The Colonel extended his hand.

"Congratulations, Steve. I mean Lieutenant Rogers."

Rogers took it very awkwardly, murmuring "Cripes," and accepting the Colonel's handshake rather cautiously, as though he had been caught out in something.

"I'll take you back to Battalion with me later," the Colonel told him, "so don't wander off."

Rogers still looked a little overcome, a little stricken. So that's it! thought Kirk.

"You'll keep your own platoon," he added.

Rogers was all grin now. The news was good news. He walked off on the heels of a crackling salute and found his men conversing in a bomb crater. He slid down among them and announced:

"I'm a Loot."

There was a brief silence.

"Did you hear that, you jokers!" a man yelled, as though he were intent on announcing it to the entire Alamein front, enemy included, "Bandy's got his pips!"

"Fog him!" replied a small, distant voice.

. . . . .

The Colonel made himself at home on a water-tin in Captain Pascoe's dug-out and faced Don Company's Commander somewhat uneasily. He decided to come straight to the point:

"Roy, Military History and Information have put in a request for you."

Pascoe's fine, nervous features came up at him sharply.

"I assume you told them they couldn't have me?"

It was half appeal.

"The Brig said he'd leave it to me. I'm leaving it to you."

"Well, you know my answer."

"Now think, and don't try any heroics. Good officers like you don't need them. Wars aren't fought only by infantry. An army's an entity, a society, and the infantry's its means of enforcing its policy. Milhist asked for you because they need you. It won't be an exactly shameful occupation, recording what we do. Our descendants might be interested."

"Well, I'm not. I'm quite content to remain Battalion historian—unless," he asked wretchedly, "you want to get rid of me?"

"For God's sake! Who the hell said anything about getting rid of you? Am I no longer to pass along a request from my Brig unless everyone turns into a sensitive plant?"

"I'm sorry, sir. I suppose I've got after-action nerves."

There had been more misery in Pascoe's tone than the conversation merited, and the Colonel watched him shrewdly.

"You're not wearing a hair shirt, are you, Roy?"

"Not that I know of. Why do you ask? Rather funny," he went on before the Colonel could reply. "Corpus Christy made the same remark."

"What's *that* brumby up to?"

"He's very quiet. Charlie Mann getting it like that shook him up a bit."

"Yes—he's sort of taken Charlie under his wing, hadn't he? Wonderful company, Corpus. He travelled with me on the railways quite a lot." Reminiscence made the Colonel look vulnerable. Also, Pascoe uncomfortable. He waited. The Colonel shook himself. "Well, he's got an M.M. I suppose I'd better tell him."

"I don't suppose a medal will help persuade him to take stripes?"

"It may," said the Colonel. "He's nothing if not unpredictable."

"The reasons he gives you for staying a private!" Pascoe burst out. "I can't help thinking he half means them too."

"I'll describe the whole scene to you," the Colonel announced with a sudden change of tone. "You approach him rather with the air of a man conferring an honour—right?"

"Right!"

"You begin: Private Christy, you are now a corporal, soon, you will be a sergeant, and, if you want it, an officer. Right?"

"Right!"

"To which our man replies something like this. I am forced to submit to the authority of colourless extroverts like Vic Kirk and of quackish intellectuals like yourself. I refuse to be bribed into submission by some trifling rank. If Kirk is a colonel and you are a captain, I should be at the least a Brigadier. If the army cares to recognise my true worth and create me General, well and good——"

"Absolutely uncanny! Someone must have repeated the entire episode to you."

"Come, Roy, you can do better than that. This used to be *my* company. Don't you think I tried to get him to take rank?"

"There's not much of *your* old company left," Pascoe stated, not looking at him.

The Colonel let it pass; in his book you didn't mention such facts. Pascoe, he noted, not for the first time, was the worrying kind. Doubts, reservations, self-questionings . . . The man's very quest for certitude made him seize on the certitude of slaughter with courage and tenacity.

Strange, he reflected, the different things that made a man a good soldier. Pascoe his torment. Christy his contempt for man-made institutions. Doc Home his sheer sensualism. Rogers his bigotry. Himself? The habit of duty over the years? The dim but pervading sense of holding something together? Personal pride? All these and something else? What had made him at the age of twenty, at Gallipoli, go up that slope against bullets coming thick as locusts? Romanticism? Male vanity? A belief in the glory of courage? Theatricality?

Did one give a damn for God, King, or Country, when one did it?

Was the "born soldier" a myth? Was it just that some tolerated it better than others? War was an unnatural state; some adapted, some rebelled or sought to evade. Some, like Pascoe, were obsessed with its idiocy and yet found relief in the very execution of war's methods. Some, like himself, found after forty-seven years that they had been the servants of a system and were called on to defend that system; and the best he could say of the system was that, imperfect as it was, its survival was justified because human decency seemed to preponderate therein.

"We're the best of a bad lot."

"I don't follow you," Pascoe was saying.

"I don't blame you. Where's Christy?"

. . . . .

"Hey, Corpus! Diddly-Dum wants you!"

The sunlight was assaulting the skin like flames by this time, and the Colonel walked with Christy towards the shade of an ammunition bay, cut into the side of the ridge where Don Company was dug in.

"Hows tricks, Arnold?"

"So-so. How's the wife?"

"A.1. They've given you the Military Medal."

"Thank them very much and send it back."

The Colonel grinned and seated himself on an ammunition box. Christy squatted opposite.

"You'll do what you're told and come and have it pinned on you along with the others."

"Care to bet?"

"Any amount you like."

Christy's grizzled hair, cut very short and never covered if he could help it, had gathered a fine golden bloom of dust. He shook it now a little despairingly.

"All this childish make-believe is not for me. Go and play your games without me."

"You wouldn't like me to get you a discharge?" suggested the Colonel helpfully.

"No, thank you. I've reconciled myself to the war and all it means, but I decline to be entangled in its gaudy sideshows. War is a ludicrous enough proposition without waving ribbons around, or engaging in ironic rites."

"So you say. Don Company performed remarkably in the action west of Jesus—the dead and the living. Let's say certain of the living have been chosen to receive honours on behalf of the Company."

"Let's say instead that certain of those fortunate or resourceful enough to survive are to be awarded bits of bunting, so the whole degrading business might be given a virtuous aspect."

"Well," said the Colonel rising, "I want to see *your* virtuous aspect at Battalion tomorrow. O-nine-hundred."

"You'll be lucky," observed Christy.

The Colonel left him. He was too old a hand to be provoked by Christy. Besides, he had his own plans.

Rogers waited beside the Colonel's jeep. The Colonel called out a farewell to Pascoe and told Rogers to mount.

"Will I be able to get transport back by nineteen hundred, sir? I'm taking out a penetrating patrol tonight."

"I think so," said the Colonel. "We're not *that* poor."

He sent the jeep leaping over the broken stones and around the end of the ridge. The plain was spread before them. Its dirty yellow surface was like a scab, with parts torn off to reveal long patches of white sand. The stunted camel thorn grew everywhere. Here and there a derelict tank rose from the desolation like a rock.

Now the land took a dip and its surface was as fine as powder. Half a mile in front of them that powder suddenly blew upwards violently, then again and again. The Colonel stopped the jeep and now they could hear the shrill passage of the shells high above their heads.

"Eighty-eights," remarked Rogers.

"How do you know they're not seventy-fives?" the Colonel asked him.

To the Colonel's surprise, Rogers gave the flippant question serious thought.

"It's just something about the shape of the explosion."

Shape of the explosion! A real old woman, Rogers, tough as he was.

"Show's over," said the Colonel a few minutes later, and put the jeep into motion again.

He wondered whether he needed to put Rogers at his ease. He recalled himself envying Rogers once or twice before the war. Rogers had a small farm a few miles outside Numerella, a tidy little place, just enough of it to keep a man going reasonably well. He had dreamed more than once of retiring to such a place. A placid, fruitful existence with animals and crops; living in the scenery instead of roaring through it beneath a banner of smoke.

"How's the farm going?" he asked Rogers abruptly.

Rogers' face lost its glumness. "Fine. I can rely on my brother, and the wife knows as much about running the place as either of us."

And one bad season could ruin you, thought the Colonel. A huge station like Ollimonto, the Stainforth property, was able to withstand the onslaught of several bad seasons; the Stainforths and others could afford to drove cattle vast distances in search of pasture and water. People like Rogers were sometimes wiped out within a matter of a few months. After the war, Rogers might very well find himself with nothing to return to. All I need do is walk into the office of the Commissioner for Railways and take up where I left off. Probably with a bit of promotion.

The Colonel swung the jeep northward, skirting the minefields, and joining the black bitumen of the narrow coast road. On their left ran the snow-white sand of the beach. The sea looked immeasurably cool and promising. The brown bodies of men bobbed in the gentle surf.

There was little traffic on the road now. By night, it would be murmurous with transport, moving up with men, ammunition, and rations to forward positions, as the Junkers droned above among the stars and tried to find the road with a stick of bombs—and sometimes did. All that was left by daylight, however, would be a few more blackened hulks on the side of the road. Sometimes they came in and straffed the road, the bullets striking brilliant blue sparks on the bitumen. By night, the arteries of the two armies began to run strongly again. They put out feelers towards each other in the darkness. Neither slept, neither was quite the same the next morning as it had been the night before.

Under the serenity of stars they shuffled, adjusted, recuperated, and replenished. Soon one or other of them would be poised and ready.

4

THE dog looked as though all the conceivable infamies had been practised on it. The eyes were protruding, motionless, and pathetic. It was spidery, and if you were to think of an actual breed of dog in relation to it, you would think of whippet. Its ribs stuck out so far, they resembled blades about to press through the coat. The hind-quarters looked as though they had been wrung out to dry.

The day before moving up to Alamein, Don Company had been bivouacing around a ruined stone building at Berg El Arab. Out of the ruins this creature had come cowering, hunched, trembling, stepping with wonderful delicacy, as though the very touch of its little feet on the earth were punishable.

Doc Home threw a stone at it, to receive a stone himself the next second, on his tin hat. Skirting Doc, the animal had gone straight to the thrower of the second stone—Christy, who was murmuring "Let him who is without sin . . ."

"It's bomb-happy," said Charlie Mann, and gave the dog half his bully-beef.

The dog gulped it down in one lump that bulged its skinny neck alarmingly.

"Poor little bastard!" marvelled Charlie. "He actually *liked* it."

The dog had remained with Don Company, except during the action round the Hill of Jesus, when it had stayed back with the support company, tied to an ammunition box. It was more or less Christy's dog; acknowledged to be under his protection, which meant something in Don Company, as Charlie Mann knew.

Doc Home had disliked the dog from the moment he saw it. To be helpless or demoralised was to invite Doc Home's contempt. Weakness in any form aroused his hatred. He knew better than to provoke the long, tireless, hard-boiled Christy, so he let the dog be.

Christy rarely called it by the same name twice. He was not sentimental about dogs. He merely upheld this creature's right of life. Besides, his championship of something so wretched seemed to him a precious assertion amidst this enormous area of destruction. It flew preposterously in the face of this gathering of men and mechanism dedicated to homicide. In his day, Christy had flown in the faces of many things. He still did.

He lay sleeping now, in his weapon-pit. The sun had crept round, for it was afternoon by this time, and half of one leg lay in its light. The dog came up from the depths of Christy's *doover*, crept along the side of the weapon-pit, and subsided mutely in the sun at Christy's foot.

Christy dreamed.

He dreamed of trees. Flarings of palm-heads stood on stilts so they might not interrupt your view of the Pacific. Camphorlaurel, kurrajong, and boabab. He went over the canefields, bent to the hot sky, up through the gorges, through the cool and dark valhallas where great begonias, tree-fern, staghorn, and orchid feasted in the mosses and the tinkling freshets. Into the ranges and the tall timber that tickled the undersides of clouds which bellowed and threw out rain. Guava, mango, hibiscus, tecoma. Silky oaks with the pearl-grey timber, rosewood, blackwood—and gum . . . They say about me that I know and name most of the five hundred varieties of gum. Manna gum, lemon gum, red gum, ghost gum; ironbark, stringybark, turpentine, and blue-gum . . . Swamp-oaks leaning to the river, like dark brushwork on the water, ti-tree and mulga——

Man is a tree. He springs towards the light and in his heyday tosses his head at the weather, then his limbs grow rotten and die, the bark begins to fall, and the wood can grow no more rings of living and finding out, the roots lose faster and faster their clutch in the earth, and a big wind comes one day to fling it finally down. Sometimes a tree bears the name of a man, a man who is dead.

The Avenue of Honour.

In the First World War the men of Numerella went away in the First Fifty-Fifth Battalion, to France and Gallipoli. Three hundred and sixty did not come back. They had joined the Fifty-Fifth from all parts of that great strip of country known as The Numerella, but they were all honoured in the town itself. The usual war memorial was erected, of course, in the middle of the wide main street, looking deadly in its utter lack of beauty; a banal, expressionless figure of a soldier that seemed to discountenance any legends of splendid courage.

Then somewhere in the folk-talk of the town was born the idea of the Avenue of Honour. A tree for every Numerella man who did not come back. In the town's conversation it became an urgency, a demand; and soon was seized on as coinage by those seeking votes, trade, contracts, or plain prestige. So it became official.

Officialdom this once failed to convert or manipulate it to its own purposes. It had solemnly set aside an area down near the river for the Avenue, but the people who had lost sons, brothers and husbands, chose the half-mile of road at the town's eastern approach, for which certain elements of officialdom had other, and selfish, plans. But it was Crown land and the Minister in Brisbane was brought to alienate a strip for the Avenue, to be held in perpetuity.

Officialdom then chose trees. Foreign trees. All the same variety to give the Avenue symmetry. The bereaved came with lemon gum, jacaranda, flowering gum, silky oak, camphorlaurel, planted, nursed, and haunted them until they struck; and at the base of each a strong stake bore a metal plate and the name of a Numerella man who had died a long way away. Finally, when they were ready, they partly mollified officialdom by allowing it to declare the Avenue open (though in which sense was never clearly explained) and to bellow platitudes into the hot sun.

So as the features of the dead grew dimmer in the memory and Anzac Day more of a habit than an expression, so did the Avenue become taller and more beautiful. The gum flowered in white, scarlet, pink, and yellow; the lemon-gum limbs went skywards slimly, taking on the hues of misty mother-of-pearl and in the summer evenings its clusters of blade-like little leaves gave off a pure odour into the air.

Twenty years after its planting, that Avenue was lovely to look on.

Then in 1939 when the talk was all of another war, a white-haired old man in a faded yellow shirt with far-back flashing eyes came down the Avenue of Honour and into the Numerella Court House. "Timothy Nilson, you are charged with assault on the person of Oswald Baillie . . ." "My name is Oswald Faulkner Baillie. I am a grazier, of Ontahoe Station, Numerella. In my spare time I am a Captain in the local Fourteenth Militia . . . On such and such a date I was acting in my capacity of Recruiting Officer for the Militia, by affixing a wooden notice—yes, your Worship, a recruiting notice—to a tree on the main road east of Numerella. Having performed this task, I was about to re-enter my car when the defendant approached, tore the notice from the tree and struck me across the head with it, rendering me unconscious . . ."

"Yes—this is what I have to say——" The old man seems to dominate the entire courtroom, the flashing of his eyes striking them all alike, as though it were lightning. "—that isn't the East Numerella Road—it's the Avenue of Honour, and don't you ever forget it——" The old man's voice is quiet now, as all the courtroom listens. "That was my brother, that tree. He died on Gallipoli in nineteen fifteen. It was a war to end wars, see. He died so that the young 'uns might go on living. That tree means peace, see. And along comes this—this animal here, and nails on a board that says there's not going to be any more peace, my brother died for nothing . . . Perhaps!" The old man's voice is loud again now. "Perhaps he did, but they shan't insult or mock him, even if he *is* just a tree on a dusty road . . . 'Cause that's the Avenue of Honour, see." The old man's tones fill the courtroom, he seems to tower, and the Magistrate, the Police, the witnesses, all forget their roles and feel as though it is they who are on trial. "The Avenue of Honour. Do you understand what I'm talking about? HONOUR!"

. . . . .

"Honour!" called Christy, and awoke.

5

THE ridges with the setting sun behind them had turned to chocolate. A great orange sun squatted just on the skyline. It seemed to have torn a hole in the sky, a hole whose edges ran with gold. The white sand glimmered, turned a restful lilac shade, shadows grew cool and found mysterious depths.

A plane sprang all black from the bowels of the sun, its guns rattling distantly; a Bren answered it perfunctorily. The plane, a Messerschmitt, swished for home above Don Company's heads. Perhaps the pilot smelt his *ersatz* coffee and felt his boots on the earth which belonged by mystical right to his own race. Perhaps he had been waiting for the flight of Hudsons on their way back from bombing Tobruk. If so, he had grown tired of it.

"Stand-to!" Pascoe called.

His company echoed the words quietly along their trenches in the dusk. Men rose to their feet and leaning on parapets looked Hunwards with a statutory air. There was a clicking of bolts, a thrusting home of magazines.

Pascoe found it strange to remember that for fifty miles tens of thousands of men were assuming attitudes of readiness and expectancy. There was a kind of terror in it, perhaps because he lived with a detached vision of the desert with men in it like crawling spots, busy striking, at declared intervals, their deathly poses.

Soon the dark would come and patrols emerge like nocturnal beasts: the endless, patient feel and counter-feel of two armies, each planning a leap at the other's throat. The moon would rise and in its light the desert would look strangely like that moon's own face.

Horrible John's voice, raucous and cynical, still addressed his fascinated audience of two:

"That joker who wrote *Till the Sands of the Desert Grow Cold* didn't know what he was talking about. They grow cold every night, cold as a nun's bum. By Christ, it useter get cold in Libya——"

"Was you in Libya, Horrible?"

"Was I in Libya? Listen, mug, you've heard of Lawrence of Arabia, haven't you?"

"Yair. Why?"

"Well, you must have heard of Jones of Libya, then."

"Can't say I have. I've heard of essence of lemon and spirits of salts."

"Yer'll hear about thickening of the ear if you aren't careful."

"Jones of Libya! Haw-haw!"

"It's gonna be Jones of Cairo soon."

"Yair and after that Jones of Jerusalem Jail."

"Pardon me, Herman."

Christy removed the dog from his greatcoat. He was currently calling it Herman because it reminded him of a wretched little German he had taken prisoner in their recent action. The animal stood there shivering, its great eyes turned up piteously to the stable element in an overwhelming world. Christy pulled his sweater from an ammunition case and knotted the sleeves around its neck. The creature sniffed the sweater and subsided into the still warm sand, its head poking forth from the garment like a mouse from its hole.

A sweater he was envied for, and had to guard. He had lifted it from an English officer back in Palestine. He used to lend it to Charlie.

Why did every damned thing come back to Charlie? As though Charlie had been the sun that the planets of one's thoughts, wandering, paused to look for in their now meaningless orbit.

It's the enormity, Pascoe was thinking. I can't seem to grasp that merciless, conglomerated reality.

What I knew and lived in up to my first minute in action that was not reality. Secure for the time in my ways, it was something around me like a cushion and a pleasant dream. I lectured to students on epochs dead and dim, of which I had only learned myself from other men's writings. What, or how much, did the collective fallibility amount to?

Perhaps Christy was right—his kind were simply ignorant: "You bloody intellectuals bore me, Roy. You gather facts as a stamp-collector collects stamps, and your heads get huge with all sorts of theories, while reality goes on all round you among the feeling and the acting people, the fallible, misused livers of life. And they are the ones who really know——"

"You disown human knowledge, Corpus?"

"No, only the intellectuals, for using it to oil their brains with and feed their conceit. I don't know which are the worst. The philosophers or the historians."

"I see," said Pascoe dryly, but with a deep inner unrest. "My kind may be only the second worst?"

"You're both bloody intellectuals," replied Christy serenely. "They're inter-dependent."

"Facts! Someone must amass the facts!" Pascoe felt desperate, finding an odd yearning in himself to earn some brand of approval from this man.

"An historian can tell the facts. Only a poet tells the truth."

Suddenly Pascoe, for the first time in his existence, had a sense of life—life as different from dynasties and institutions. Life not in *isms*, epochs or ages; but the fury to live and the appetite to destroy. The sheer act of being. It was as though he had by some miracle acquired in that second an alien language.

"Is that why you write poetry?" he asked.

Christy shrugged and said wryly:

'There's only occasional poetry in all the words I wrote. You want to talk to Charlie Mann. That boy at twenty perceives more of the wordless truths than I——"

"Wordless?"

"Wordless in the sense that only a poet knows the words. I feel these truths and seldom have words, but Charlie can look at a thing and the words are there as though some hidden source has been tapped."

It wasn't just a son Christy had seen in Charlie Mann; Christy had seen some other self. Charlie had the makings of someone that Christy had wanted—or striven—to be. And what was Christy now? A man approaching middle-age who had rejected all ambition, distrusted the human mind profoundly, and despised institutions. An occasionally published poet—Pascoe recalled him being referred to by a literary magazine—one of those "intellectual" things he despised—as a "primitive". He had jeered at Christy about this.

"Literary magazines!" Christy thundered. "Intellectuals hanging like leeches on to the belly of talent and genius. As if a poet can't warble without some bloody literary analyst taking each line to pieces. You can't take a scalpel to the soul."

Christy had had the intelligence and the personality to take him to the top—even as a self-chosen private in the Fifty-Fifth he was a kind of power. Here am I, thought Pascoe, in charge of a department at thirty, probably a professorship in ten years; twice a Fellow at Oxford—seeking his approval, probing the reasons for his contempt . . . He looked across at Christy in a near-by trench, in the deepening dusk. I'll talk with him again tonight, he thought. In the meantime Rogers was taking out a penetrating patrol; a routine sort of thing of twelve men, four from each platoon, so no one platoon could complain of being overworked.

"Corpus!" he called. "You aren't going out on patrol tonight are you?"

He allowed each platoon commander to choose the four men

himself, and he could not remember the names handed to him for the moment.

Christy shook his head. Pascoe gloated. He thought he had a remark to confound Christy.

Brunette, dreamed Doc Home. Long neck, slim shoulders, small breasts, long hips sweeping down to buttocks like a pair of light-globes, the legs long too and the very light stockings running straight up the Achilles tendon with their seams bisecting the legs all the way up to the thighs . . . He'd feed her brandy. He adored women in drink, the wanton, slavish look they got into their eyes.

Horrible John had lowered his voice for, in process of providing thumbnail sketches of Don Company personnel for the two new men, he had arrived at Doc Home.

"Don't ever come the raw prawn with Doc, mate. He knows all the lurks. Done most things. Doc has. Especially where there's good dough for not much work, and especially where there's sheilas around. He's a bad bastard with sheilas. Once, a few years ago, he nearly went to jug for having corporal knowledge of a schoolgirl. But let me tell yers about when he used to work in the morgue. They used to bring in bodies with no identification—you know, old swaggies who'd died on the track, or bludgers picked up dead from metho. Well, old Doc used to sell them to medical blokes and pocket the dough himself. He did all right, I'll tell yers."

They heard the sound of the Hudsons coming back. They sailed out of the north-west, fairly low, in uneven formation.

"Two missing," someone remarked.

They passed over, and in a few minutes were lost to sight, and only a drone behind them. "Two gone," the voice repeated.

Over a ridge a Hudson came very slowly, one engine hanging brokenly, like a ponderous bird looking for somewhere to alight. The entire company was silent as it watched.

The Hudson dropped lower and lower, skimming the flat desert.

"Hold it, mate," somebody implored.

"They're over minefields there!"

A purple, labouring shadow, coughing and snarling at the tranquil dusk. What rended them about this? thought Christy. They saw death daily, saw it come to men they knew. Why, I have to remind myself there *are* men inside of her. The death of a piece of machinery; that was what they saw—and it was unutterably moving.

The Hudson touched the desert and in the same instant was lost in a sudden great boiling of sooty smoke and a flash. Fragments of steaming metal bounced over the desert on the heels of the explosion. The black smoke boiled lower and small flames seemed to be sucking greedily at its belly. The smoke was diffused and mingled with the dusk, part of the sky's chemistry, part of the infinite.

Plane, men, all one, all disintegrated in one searing flash—a bang, a chemical change . . . Death of a plane . . . And soon, thought Christy, the human chain began its reaction: reports, notifications, right back to homes, rooms, beds, where women knew that if they were ever going to worry again, it must be about another man. The desert could never get enough blood and the woman would have to seek new love, a new father for her child . . . *There are three things that are never satisfied. The grave and the barren womb; the earth that is not filled with water.*

"Well, at least," came Horrible John's voice, "they never knew what hit them."

The last edge of the sun outlined the ridge, and was gone. Now was the time for patrols before the moon came up too far. Men began to be busy in the gloom. Rogers gathered his twelve men. Check equipment. Did they have everything clear? This was the bearing. This was the object.

They passed, murmuring, Don Company's forward sentry. "The challenge is 'Whose kelpie's that?' The password is 'Whiskers Blake's.' Just in case yers come home tonight."

"We will. We promised Mother."

"Much doing? What sort of a patrol is it anyway?"

A voice answered the sentry pompously:

"We are about to inspect the installations of that well-known organisation, the Afrika Corps."

"Fog Hitler," said the sentry.

6

CHRISTY went back to the depths of his *doover*, followed by the dog. It slid down trailing its master's sweater. Christy fed it a slab of bully-beef. He had made his own lamp of an empty tobacco tin, filled with stolen kerosene, a strip of webbing for a wick, enclosed by perspex taken from a crashed plane. He hung a blanket over the entrance of the coffin-like dwelling and lit the lamp. The dog licked its meagre chops and settled in a corner where he could watch his sun, moon, and stars.

The lord of the manor next began to look for his chameleon. That, too, he had come across in the stones of Berg El Arab. There was an end of string tied to a nail, and following the string several feet among the roof-iron of the *doover* he found the chameleon, now a dark chocolate hue. As he brought it into the light it went dirty yellow and swivelled its ancient-looking eyes. From a matchbox, he tipped out a little pile of dead insects in front of the chameleon. That done, he reclined in the sand beneath the niche where the lamp burned. He took out a sheet of paper headed "July 31st, 1942." Beneath it he wrote "Black August."

The first stanza came quickly:

"Now this black August draws upon us,
The dust is starred with ruin and its breath is rotten;
The line is straight, the dead lie out upon the ridges;
August is on us and Tobruk is best forgotten."

Charlie would never wear a tin hat; always the old felt hat blackened by sweat, right over on one side of the head, and with a brigandish air. It seemed to suit the laughing face. Christy began to write again, more slowly, less assuredly, leaving spaces. Yes, something about the hat and a laughing face:

"Recalling in a crumpled tilt past light of eyes that
    sleep . . .
. . . an old felt hat which I shall keep . . ."

Of course, he could give way to this feeling of savage irony and write something about:

"I've only this to say of him: There is
Some corner of this poisonous dust,
Immaculate beaches, glowing sea,
Wreck, wire, ruin, racket,
That is for ever Charlie . . ."

"Corpus!" said a soft voice, and Pascoe came through the blanket. "*Timeo Danaos et dona ferentes.* I've got half a bottle of whisky the old man slipped me."

The white sand was glowing now in the full-grown night. White stars sprinkled a black sky. An occasional Very light soared like a wayward comet, lit up some strip of landscape in a ghastly glimmer, and died again.

Being in support, the company had only one man in each platoon standing sentry. There were minefields and forward posts screening them from the enemy, and any attack.

Some of them had donned greatcoats and still lay out on the sand, preferring the rapidly chilling air to the stuffy *doovers*. Horrible John still held court to the new men:

"You shoulda seen the trick Doc played on old Herbie Tonks from C Company. Just after we came out of Tobruk last year, it was. Doc and old Herbie were in the same leave party to Jerusalem. Well, the moment he got off the leave bus Herbie started to punish the grog. Only saw him twice we did, in five days, and each time he was so blotto he couldn't scratch himself.

"Well, going back to camp in the bus Herbie was sitting next to Doc and feeling awful crook with the grog, shaking and groaning and holding his head and telling Doc he was going to die. 'Well, die yer bastard,' says Doc. I never saw anyone who was feeling Captain Cook get any sympathy from Doc.

"You know how the Wogs mark their sheep, don't you? They stain them different colours to pick their flocks out. Well, we pass a lot of fields near Rehovot with these sheep scattered all over them, and all these sheep had big stains of colour on them—all the colours of the rainbow.

"Herb gives an awful groan. 'What's wrong now?' asks Doc. 'Look at them fields over there,' whispers Herbie. 'Do you see pink and purple and orange and green animals walking all over them?' Doc looks out the window. 'All I see's an old camel,' Doc tells him. 'Oh, Gawd!' screams Herbie. 'I've got them. I've got the D.T.s!' They had to hold him down all the rest of the journey."

. . . . .

"So you say," murmured Christy, "that my attitude has a psychological basis· Yes, Freud and Jung have been wonderful pools for you to paddle in, haven't they?" He upended the canteen and swallowed some whisky. As he smacked his lips the dog raised its head and watched Christy anxiously. "You theorise that my declared contempt for the intellectual has its basis in my lack of education. Let me tell you that I rejected education. I am compensating for nothing that I ever went short of. Man has been acquiring more and more knowledge and becoming at the same time more and more destructive. Why? Because morality is not a matter of theory or dogma or doctrine. It can no more be captured between the pages of a text-book than poetry. Christianity began as a creed for which men died gladly. It married the state and became the right arm of oppression and conquest. 'Civilise with syphilis, Bibles and whips!' The intellectual *élite* who in the name of a doctrine invented the war we now find ourselves in. Whatever the tyranny, Communism, Fascism, howling behind the tyrants you will find a pack of intellectuals ready to find sound moral reasons for any infamy. Knowledge has so corrupted them they have forgotten how to think morally. Intellectuals are the curse of the twentieth century."

"What am I now?" Pascoe asked, a note of almost hysterical appeal in his voice. "I have been de-intellectualised. I no longer think intellectually. My whole concept of life has been so altered that I fear I may never return to what I was. Therefore," he ended, pouring Christy more whisky, "what am I?"

"Here—what are any of us?" said Christy. "We are voices talking in an empty room in a language we have forgotten the meaning of. We have no meaning, except as agents of mutual destruction."

. . . . .

"Whose kelpie's that?"

"Whiskers Blake's," a voice said quietly from the darkness.

"Come on in," said the sentry.

The patrol came through the wire, riflemen, Bren-gunners,

tommy-gunners; finally two men who carried a form between them.

They laid the form on the ground and somebody covered the face with a greatcoat.

"Who is it?" asked the sentry.

"Steve Rogers."

7

"WELL!" asked Pascoe harshly. "How did it happen?"

Rogers's Corporal swallowed, with an accused air.

"They must have seen us on our way in, sir, and let us through. They ambushed us on the way back. Lieutenant Rogers got the full issue on their first burst. They withdrew when we opened fire ourselves."

"All right," said Pascoe kindly. "Don't take it personally. Go and get some sleep."

The corporal left the Company dug-out where Pascoe had returned. He sat down and was suddenly afraid of being alone. Voices in an empty room talking in a language we no longer know the meaning of . . .

In the history books war made sense, because the historians *made* it make sense. He recalled the sensuous delight he had taken in describing the sweep of Napoleon's armies over the face of Europe. In the conquests of imperial Spain he had seen only a richness and a majesty of deed.

What did the case of Steve Rogers mean in history? A decent, devoted man, shot down dead a few hours after getting a merited commission. Yet such things were the daily truths of war. Ah, truth. That was for the poets like Christy and the late Charlie Mann.

War perhaps only made sense in its reality to the megalomaniacs like Hitler and Stalin and Mussolini, to the sadists like Doc Home or the adroit betrayers up top. And afterwards to the historians, to the intellectual who found the soundest of moral reasons for every infamy. Did it follow therefore that war was an unhuman condition? It had to follow. Perhaps he had at least found the true reason why Christy had refused to accept a Military Medal. He refused to participate in the hypocrisy of giving a human or emotional aspect to a non-human thing.

He felt certain now that he would repeat that dream he could not remember, only by the awakening it carried. Always the question. He awoke in that dug-out like a man buried alive and the question enclosed him like a horrible infested skin, all over him: *What was it all for? What did it all mean?*

And yet the dream of which the question was the aftermath always eluded him.

Like someone fighting for air, he came out again into the night. The moon had risen and re-made the desert in its own image. Stars had set and others risen. The earth turned. The sea went its way. *And what did Rogers matter?* Except to one of the new men who was talking of it as though the killing of Rogers was an injustice which could be brought home to some one person. Except to Christy, answering gently:

"Death has no tact."

When the body was carried past Christy's *doover* the dog set up a howling. Christy quietened it, but it came out, still trailing the sweater, and followed the body. When the body was finally laid to rest in a spare *doover*, covered in a blanket, the dog sat outside, still grieving. Neither stones nor shouts dismissed it.

"What's wrong with that mong?" someone complained.

"It's come out in sympathy," Horrible John told him.

The moon went away again. Pascoe sat making out situation reports and wished he had not shared so much whisky with Christy.

All sounds in the dead hours seemed to come from a great distance. Transport, an insect hum, gunfire like snores, and mortars the plopping of corks out of some spectral bottle.

An hour before dawn, Horrible John came from his trench in a greatcoat with a haversack upon his arm and his rifle slung. He walked casually to the defecation trench. Having made sure he was not observed, he removed his tin hat and brought from the greatcoat pocket a crumpled felt hat, which he donned. He stuck his rifle in the sand by the bayonet and hung the tin hat on the butt. Then he walked swiftly away. Once he turned round to look at the symbol he had left standing next to the trench. He grinned. Why not?

He was dead to the army from this moment on.

8

JUST on first light the sentry came back from the wire and woke Pascoe, who had not long fallen asleep. Pascoe woke his runner.

"Stand-to."

The runner rose shivering and went away on his errand. Heads and shoulders rose from trenches to blot the lightening sky. Small noises multiplied. It was bitterly cold. A cruel little wind came off the sea.

"Hey, mate," one of the new men whispered to Christy, "Horrible John's gone."

"Gone where?"

"I dunno. But he was reckoning yesterday he was going to shoot through."

"There's a Pommy ack-ack mob just over the ridge," Christy told him. "You'll find him over there looking for loot."

The sky above the ridges in the east glimmered like dirty silver until the ridges grew a pure, shining edge. These edges bared black teeth, which became as the light grew brighter, the silhouettes of tanks and armoured cars, moving very slowly, off on some nameless dawn patrol.

The stand-to lasted half an hour, by which time the desert lay leaden but clear in the light. From the anti-aircraft unit he had just mentioned Christy had acquired some days earlier a tin of bacon, which he now opened and began to fry the contents thereof in his trench shovel, over the flame of his lamp. A pin-point of domesticity in the deadly and lachrymose landscape. Strangely human. A pathos. Almost a sentimentality.

It was Doc Home who found Horrible John's symbol at the defecation trench. He grinned when he recognised the J.J. scratched on the hat. Lowering his shorts, he squatted above the trench and regarded the symbol thoughtfully as he relieved himself. When he had finished he rose, took the tin hat from the rifle butt and dropped it into the trench.

"That's where that belongs."

He withdrew the rifle from the sand and examined it. It was cocked, the safety-catch released, and a round in the breach. As he extracted the round he murmured to himself:

"Careless bastard."

• • • • •

By eight o'clock the sun was hot. Two trucks arrived from Battalion Headquarters: one a small desert-buggy for Rogers, the other a thirty-hundredweight, containing the Regimental Provost Sergeant and two of his men.

The Provost Sergeant was called Arthur Bastable, an unfortunate name for someone in his position.

The three provosts went first to Pascoe's *doover*. What transpired there seemed to leave Pascoe almost beside himself with amusement. He watched as the three provosts made towards Christy's slit-trench.

Christy was feeding the dog when he became conscious of the three forms on his parapet. He looked up.

"Private Christy—you're under close arrest.'

Christy was on the point of turning away, when he decided that Bastable meant it. The Provost Sergeant was looking his most regimental and the other two had nervously unbuttoned the holster-flaps of their .38's. Seeing Bastable obviously anticipated an indignant question, Christy said nothing, but patted the dog, donned his tin hat, picked up his tommy-gun and joined his three captors.

"Lead on—Sergeant Barst-able."

They took him towards the thirty-hundredweight. Suddenly the watching Pascoe felt shoddy. There was something symbolic about Christy's silence and dignity.

"What have you done?" someone called to Christy.

"I sold latrine plans to Rommel," replied the prisoner.

He climbed aboard with his escort close behind, both looking completely at a loss. Christy composed himself on the floor of the truck and the Sergeant and his two men got between Christy and the tailboard.

"Why don't you travel in the cabin, Sergeant? I shan't try to escape."

"Orders," said Bastable.

He tapped on the back of the cabin and the truck lurched into motion. There was silence but for the engine. Christy smoked, and lay back with his tin hat over his face. Suddenly, one of the men could bear it no longer.

"For Christ's sake! Don't you want to know what it's all about?"

Christy raised the hat and regarded him mildly:

"If it makes you any happier, yes. Sergeant, why have I been arrested?"

Bastable drew himself as stiff as the unsteady truck would allow him, and snapped:

"To go and get decorated!"

9

Padre Stringer of the Fifty-Fifth was a fairly commonplace man, with black eyebrows, deep-set eyes, and a heavily creased forehead giving him a look of intensity which he did not reflect in his soul. He also had a tight, strained voice and a prophetic shock of hair. When he spoke his lips puckered, so that all told, he could utter clerical platitudes and yet sound as though he were calling down judgments, scouring sinners, and opening up visions of hellfire. Christy had dubbed him Apocalypse Pete, but this had been misheard by most of the other ranks and repeated as Puckerlips. The Padre thus blamed Christy for saddling him with a malicious nickname. Christy had never troubled to disabuse him.

A simple man, he had once believed himself a fundamentalist. He had never married because he had not so far met a woman who would agree with her husband giving most of his substance to the poor. In fact, he had been in the habit of giving money, clothes, and food to any who came to him and expressed want. The shrewder minds among the other ranks had long ago put him down as a "soft touch" for money. He had listened with compassion to many a fantasy told by rogues coming freshly fleeced from the two-up ring or the poker school.

Soon after coming into the army he had decided that he was not functioning according to his principles. He had been a declared pacifist. Despite the necessity to oppose Fascism he could not escape the feeling that he must, as a pacifist, oppose violence in all places. In short, he had no right to be giving comfort or guidance to men who were habitually bloody. He had to assure the men at regular intervals of the righteousness of their cause, yet he could not help thinking that there were ministers of religion saying exactly the same to the Germans. The Nazi soldiers needed spiritual guidance as much as the Australian—probably more, seeing what Hitler had converted them to. He once had a wild vision of himself walking into the German lines to exhort them to lay down their arms.

He had bravely divided himself. He functioned in sorrow as the padre, which no one noticed, for he was habitually glum, and created for himself a world of private penance, wherein he kept his fundamentalism, like a bud on an apparently dead bough, awaiting the spring. The men were not to know that his generosity with money and other things was not mere "softness". He was functioning, at least in one sense, as he thought he should.

Christy had clashed with him twice, and each time had humiliated him. The first time was over saluting officers.

At the end of 1941, when the Australians had come back to the fleshpots of Palestine after eight months' siege in Tobruk, and descended riotously upon the cities, British officers, not yet wise in the ways of diggers, had expected, and even demanded, salutes from Australians as well as from their own men.

Christy and Charlie Mann were accosted one day in Jerusalem by a British captain and ordered to pay the customary courtesy to the King's uniform. Wooden-faced, they obliged. The officer went on, congratulating himself on having shown at least two of these damned Australians what discipline was. Around the next corner he met the same two Australians, who disrupted pedestrian traffic by lining up on the pavement and dealing out text-book salutes. He was torn between suspicion and vanity. By the time he had encountered the same two men in a bar, a cafe, two shops, and in the tortuous streets of the Old City, and each time found his way blocked by two stonily saluting men, he was all certainty. He began to ignore them; then at last found himself confronted by an Australian provost sergeant to whom the two persecutors were complaining that he had failed to honour the King's uniform by returning a salute. The provost had taken the captain aside and told him kindly, "Look, sir, let me give you a bit of advice. Either take your cap off, or go and take refuge in the Officers' Club. And, sir, don't bother about the saluting. They don't mean any offence to the King's uniform really. Just ignore them when you see any, and thank God they're sober and behaving themselves."

A British major had accosted Doc Home, then a corporal, and Horrible John in Tel Aviv, with the same demand. A horrible comedy ensued. Doc wriggled like an embarrassed schoolgirl and dug Horrible in the ribs:

"Go on, Horrible, give the nice man a salute."

Horrible John, writhing with bashfulness and wrapping one bare, beefy leg around the other, hung his head and gurgled:

"No, I'm too shy. You give him one."

"Oh, I couldn't really," Doc crooned girlishly. "Go on, you give the nice man one."

By this time a crowd had collected, for it happened to be Allenby Road: Jews, Arabs, Tommies and other Australians—to enjoy this travesty of femininity. And Doc and Horrible John went on coyly wriggling and telling each other in witless falsettos to "give the nice man a salute".

Two more unsuitable imitators of girlhood could never again be found, and it was probably the best piece of free entertainment that Allenby Road ever saw. The major, blushing like a girl himself by this time, fled.

However, the Major had not been altogether demoralised. Complaining to Australian Liaison, he described the two men's colour patches and mentioned that they called each other "Doc" and "Horrible". The complaint ended up on Colonel Kirk's desk. First, and in private, he told the major it served him bloody well right and in future to leave his men alone when they were on leave after eight months in Tobruk. Then he put Doc and Horrible in charge of the bellowing Sergeant Bastable for a week's saluting practice. In so doing, he paid off a number of old scores, and Doc and Horrible John knew it. So they took it quietly. Besides, they got their ration of fun out of the humourless Bastable.

It all came to a head when Australian Army Headquarters put out a routine order about unit commanders tightening up on saluting. The Colonel called in Padre Stringer.

Traditionally, when an infantry commander has need of erudition, he summons the Padre. He asked Padre Stringer to write out for him the origins of saluting, in order that he might convince the men there was nothing degrading in saluting an officer. The result was that a routine order came out to the effect that in future all members of the Fifty-Fifth would salute officers between sunrise and sunset, at the same time informing the Battalion: "The origins of saluting are by no means degrading or humiliating. Saluting originated either in the Age of Chivalry, when knights raised their visors to identify each other; or at the Court of Queen Elizabeth, where history records that the male courtiers were in the habit of shading their eyes with a hand when the Queen approached, as if dazzled by her beauty." The Colonel thought the Padre had done very well.

Next morning found all notice boards in the Battalion lines carrying the following addendum to the latest routine order: "There is a greater body of historical evidence that saluting began in medieval times as the pulling of forelocks by serfs in the presence of the Lord who owned their bodies and souls. The origins therefore are both humiliating and degrading, and contradict the principles for which our Padre alleges us to be fighting." The handwriting was Christy's.

From then on, men had the habit of whipping off their hats when approaching an officer and pulling a forelock. Stainforth was all for charges and mass confinement to barracks; the Colonel preferred to let it die a natural death. He had more important orders to worry over. The Fifty-Fifth had been ordered to the Turkish border. Too many German agents were getting over to Aleppo. There might be trouble.

The second challenge was against something more fundamental than the Padre's erudition.

Most soldiers regarded Church Parade as a necessary evil; or an unholy compromise, by which the soldier is allowed to do more or less nothing, except sing and pray, and sits while the Padre recommends moral standards which the army itself renders impossible. The soldier doesn't mind being bored as long as he is at rest; he is used to boredom. But to bore Christy was as good as offering insult. Hence the Strict Heathens.

Christy and five others had ducked a Church Parade and when charged and paraded to the Colonel, Christy as the spokesman had explained that there was nothing in Army Law to compel a soldier to go to Divine Service.

"Quite so," agreed Kirk—then suddenly snapped: "The charge against the six of you, however, is that you failed to attend a *parade*—and you will attend each and every parade I choose to call, whether it's a Church Parade or a parade for the purpose of standing on your heads. Seven days' C.B.!"

The first round went to the Colonel. Stopping Christy in the lines afterwards, he asked:

"What's wrong with you, Corpus? That wasn't a very smart move. I expected something more subtle from you."

"Wait and see," murmured Christy.

The Colonel sighed. "You know who always wins these tussles, don't you?"

"There are three types of victory," retorted Christy. "Physical, moral, and Pyrrhic."

"To hell with morals! This is a war!"

Christy winked. "Quite so."

"Get out of my bloody sight!" laughed Kirk. A few minutes

after this encounter, it came to him that Christy had inadvertently shown him the true meaning of a then significant word. French Resistance. Norwegian Resistance. Dutch Resistance. That intangible that no occupying power, however ruthless, could get its hands on. Resistance. Perhaps Christy should have been in an Underground somewhere, or in some guerilla force scurrying round mountains. Damn him!

The Strict Heathens dutifully attended Church Parade the following Sunday and marched off with the rest of Don Company to the Y.M.C.A. hut where Divine Service was held. At the door of the hut the Strict Heathens about turned and marched in an opposite direction.

"Halt those men!" yelled the R.S.M.

The men halted. The R.S.M. came hotly up to them:

"And just where do you lot think you are going?"

"Back to our tents, Sar-Major," explained Christy innocently.

"Oh-ho." The R.S.M. rocked on his heels, tapping his stick on the back of a calf as he regarded his old enemy with calculation. "By whose orders, Private Christy?"

"By our soldiers' rights, Sar-Major. We cannot be compelled to attend a religious ceremony against our consciences."

"You lot with consciences!" the R.S.M. bellowed. "That's new, that is!"

The Heathens waited.

"Well, now," proceeded the R.S.M. with an awful grin, "we'll have to find something to occupy your minds while we're in there Bible-bashing, won't we?"

"Oh, Gawd," whispered one of the Heathens.

"Report to the Orderly Sergeant," crooned the R.S.M. "You can do a little latrine duty."

"I wish to be paraded to the C.O. immediately after Church Parade," retorted Christy at once. "You are victimising us for our disbelief."

"Yes, that's right," agreed the R.S.M. delightedly.

But he paraded Christy after the service, knowing better than to put himself in the legal wrong with Christy. The Colonel called up reserves. He appeared in his office with Padre Stringer. Even Christy looked taken aback.

"Now!" began the Colonel briskly. "I've brought the Padre in, because I think it's up to you six men to tell him, man to man, why you object to attending Divine Service. There's no need for me to tell you not to all speak at once. As sure as night follows day, Christy here is about to speak up on your behalf."

Christy ignored the Padre and addressed the Colonel.

"I did not get paraded for the purpose of theological discussion with the Padre. Why we don't choose to attend Service is a matter for our conscience alone." A stifled noise from the R.S.M. there. "What we wish to complain about is the R.S.M.'s attempt to victimise us for our disbelief. The Christians enjoy being humiliated for their principles. We don't."

The Colonel looked aside expectantly at the Padre.

"Aren't you a Christian?" Stringer asked Christy.

"Of course I'm not! Would I be here, in the army, if I were?"

The Padre felt his heart go small and cold. In that moment he feared Christy. They were all looking at him to reply to Christy. He wanted to run out of the Colonel's office, away from the camp, away from himself. At last he said wretchedly:

"I want no man at my services if his attendance is against his conscience." He raised his voice. He could be at least part Christian. "I ask, sir, that these men are not given unpleasant duties for not attending service. That," he added looking directly at Christy, "would offend *my* conscience."

"I'm afraid your charity's misplaced," the Colonel commented grimly. "However, I'll respect your wishes." He turned with a quietly savage air to the Strict Heathens. "Don't I pray you, for their own sakes, recommend this caper to the other men. If it catches on, I'll have the whole bloody battalion on an all-day route march. During all future Church Parades, you'll stay in your tents and put them in inspection order. The Sar-Major will inspect them, and if he finds one speck of dust, one wrongly arranged piece of gear, he'll report it to me, and I shall demonstrate the true meaning of the word 'bastard'." He paused for breath. "And now, Sar-Major, get the six of them out of this building. The Second World War, as far as I know, is still in progress."

10

WHEN the news was circulated at Battalion Headquarters that morning, that Christy was on his way to be decorated, under close arrest, Stainforth and his faithful Price-Gore were openly gratified. Major Brand, the Second in Command, remarked that "Christy would make some sort of capital out of it".

Stringer himself was aware of a mean little maggot of elation. Christy had sat in the seat of the scornful once too often. Stringer was going to watch every second of this ceremony.

The small bowl of dead ground where Battalion Headquarters was situated was like an open-air theatre. All the B.H.Q. personnel were there to watch, sitting around the stony slopes looking both curious and shocked. The R.S.M. had kept them at a distance from the Colonel's Headquarters dug-out, so that they could only see, and not hear.

The truck swept in on a dust-cloud. The tail-board came down and the escort jumped down and motioned Christy to follow. He stood quietly and expressionlessly between his two guards. Bastable went off to tell the Colonel of his arrival. A few seconds later the Colonel came above ground.

Suddenly the Padre was at Kirk's side.

"Victor, you can't do this to Christy."

The Colonel blinked a little after the gloom of the dug-out.

"Just watch me," he replied.

"I put it to you that the man has reasons of conscience for his attitude."

"He always has," said Kirk grimly. "And I'm not interested in consciences."

Far, far above a reconnaissance plane circled like a silver promise of heaven to come. The men watching from a distance were very quiet.

"This is *my* battalion," said the Colonel. "Not Christy's. If G.H.Q. see fit to decorate a member of *my* battalion, I'm going to see that it's accepted."

"I shan't watch."

"Then go and pray for him!" said the Colonel savagely.

They had both turned away, and the Colonel stepped back to Stringer and spoke desperately.

"Peter, old friend—forget I ever said such a thing."

"It's forgotten," said Stringer.

The Colonel was trembling. As he approached the prisoner the trembling increased and he paused to control it. Recovered, he began to walk briskly towards Christy. He was wearing his decorations, something he rarely did: the Military Cross and D.C.M. of his own that he had won on Gallipoli twenty-seven years earlier.

• • • • •

The truck had gone back to Don Company, Christy in the back, a ribbon on his ragged shirt, a free man, his gun restored to him.

"Well," asked the Padre, "how did the hero take it?"

"Never batted an eyelid," said the Colonel.

"Didn't he say anything?"

"Yes, five words exactly: *I'm wearing this for Charlie.*"

INTENTION

11

"THE provosts caught Jones a few miles down the road," said Major Brand, coming into Kirk's dug-out with a message form in his hand. "Any comments for Brigade?"

"None," said the Colonel. "He's past my help now. This is desertion in the face of the enemy. I suppose Roy Pascoe will have to go along and give evidence at the Court Martial."

"What will he get?"

"Life, I hope . . . One of my men running out like that!"

"Horrible John wouldn't understand the ethics of it," Brand laughed, and went back out to the large timber-propped hole in the ground known as the Orderly Room.

Jones wouldn't dare show his face in Numerella after the war, thought Kirk. Or would he? The stigma wouldn't bother Horrible John. Jones had no pride of the Fifty-Fifth, no pride of Numerella. He wasn't even fit to be called a Numerella man. Is that why I'm indifferent to what becomes of him? Kirk asked himself.

He was still asking it when the Don R came from Brigade with the signal marked Most Secret. He called Brand in as he was tearing the message open. When he had read it, he said to his Second in Command:

"The battalion's yours for a while, Joe. I'm wanted at Brigade. Divisional conference."

"I knew all this peace was too good to last," Brand commented gloomily.

The Colonel took up his tin hat, his binoculars and his map-case, and going out into the Orderly Room, told Price-Gore to summon his driver and jeep. A few minutes later Kirk was climbing in beside the driver saying: "Brigade."

The jeep swung out on to the tarred road and the driver sent it flying along to get the wind in their faces.

"That true about Horrible John Jones?" he asked the Colonel.

"What?"

"About him shooting through from the line and getting picked up by the provosts."

"True enough."

"They'll be solid on him for that, won't they?"

"He's gone," agreed the Colonel.

"A bad bastard, Horrible," commented the driver. As if in extenuation, he murmured: "Funny man though."

The Colonel grunted. He was still absorbed in guesswork about this summons to Brigade.

. . . . .

At Brigade there was a provost specially on duty to direct him to a big Indian-type tent, dug in with the roof at ground level and camouflaged with a mixture of paint and sand. There was another provost on guard at the entrance, and Kirk, ducking his head to get through the flap, straightened up inside, and knew the worst. Something big was on and the Fifty-Fifth was to be right in the middle of it. Ken Wills, his Brigade Commander was there, with two British Staff Officers, both Colonels, and the folding tables set up in the tent had ten chairs around them.

"Here's Kirk now," said Wills coming forward. He was a huge, black-haired man with flashing teeth, more like an Italian singer than a first-class soldier. "Kirk, of the Fifty-Fifth Australian, Madden and Fenwick of Corps Headquarters."

Kirk shook hands with the two Englishmen, hardly noticing which name belonged to which Corps!

Ten chairs, he thought. They probably expected two more Australian Battalion Commanders, an Artillery officer, and perhaps some tank men and an Air Liaison officer. Looked like a Brigade stink.

He was a long way out.

There came Wills's Brigade Major, two Australian Staff Officers from Division, Gorman of the Artillery, then right on Gorman's heels, Manfield, one of the surviving Australian Generals in the Middle East. No other Australian Battalion Commanders.

Manfield was a small, slim, quiet man. He murmured to the company to be seated, and at his call his A.D.C., and a Captain who was not even introduced to them, brought in a large map which they hung at the end of the tent. Manfield began to speak, and as he listened Kirk felt like a man who had struggled up from the depths of a nightmare to find himself reliving it in reality.

12

"Stop the jeep!" called the Colonel. The driver glanced sideways at him in surprise. What was wrong with the old coot, telling him to stop here? The driver smiled obligingly and applied his brakes. The rush of the wind died and in its place they heard the sea, two hundred yards down on their right. The driver looked inquiringly at his commander.

"Let's get some sea air," said the Colonel.

They jumped on to the ground. It was late afternoon. The white beach was deserted, there was a moderate surf running.

"How about a dip?" suggested the driver.

"You can," the Colonel told him. "I'll give you fifteen minutes. I'll sit up on the sandhill here. I've got a military problem to think out."

The driver began to strip.

"Need any advice?" he asked.

Kirk grinned. "I'll call if I get stuck."

The driver ran naked down the slope of sand and threw himself with a whoop into the surf. He swam out for fifty yards, then looked back at the beach. The Colonel was a hunched, unmoving figure against the black road. What was wrong with him? Probably a bit crooked about Horrible John shooting through in the line. Letting Numerella down. He supposed Diddly-Dum was pretty proud of his rifle companies. Seemed to think the light shone out of their arses.

Kirk relived the scene in the tent at Brigade with great thoroughness. The Numerella Show they were going to call it. It was simple. It was logical. It was bloody murder . . . "This is the plan, Colonel . . ."

• • • • •

The German armour was concentrated in the south, keeping up the pressure on that dangerous bulge in the Eighth Army's front. The problem: Get that armour up to the north without shifting too much of our own, in order that the bulge can be straightened up by the British armour. That meant feinting in the north. That meant luring the German armour up by putting on a very convincing show. The Fifty-Fifth, with a little help, was going to put on the show.

By the time they were ready to attack, the Germans would have been given the impression that an attack on a brigade front with heavy armoured support was being mounted. Dummy tanks were to be put up all behind the Brigade area. Companies from other brigades would be brought up in daylight, then taken back under cover of dark. The actual attack would be carried out by the Fifty-Fifth alone, strung across a brigade front with nothing more in the way of armoured support than a Jock column. Simultaneously the armour would start to push in the south.

This was the first statement of intention, as given to him by one of the British Staff officers. Manfield then began to elaborate. He did so carefully, as if to talk his way round the shock in Kirk's mind. The whole thing depended on the Germans believing wholeheartedly in the bluff. The Jock column would be widely deployed and kick up a lot of dust. The Fifty-Fifth had to go in as though there were a brigade intent on making a large bulge in the German front. Short as the operation would be, it must be fought hard enough to keep the Germans convinced for one day, after which the armour in the south ought to have done its work—and the Fifty-Fifth could then "find its own way home".

Manfield spoke these last words factually; once the blow had been struck in the south and the Fifty-Fifth had to get out as best it could. He put it neither grandly, nor apologetically. It was a thing to be done and the Fifty-Fifth, his favourite battalion, was to do it. Manfield glanced at the Englishmen to carry it on from there, then found that everybody was looking at Kirk.

The Colonel was not only surprised at his words, but ashamed, as he sat there on the sandhill recalling them, of their bitterness:

"In short, you're going to make a decoy duck of my Battalion."

As though, thought Kirk wryly, I had some proprietary claim and the Fifty-Fifth, with its enormous fighting ability, were a commodity over which I had sole retail rights. It was a jealous, petty remark, and Manfield wisely did not meet it full on. All he said was:

"The Fifty-Fifth can do it."

Both a tribute—and a sentence.

One by one, they demolished his objections. He did not speak them as objections, but in his heart, objections they certainly were.

"Reinforcements?"

"No—sorry. We're scouring the training battalions, but those men are to be held back. We want only battle-hardened men for this show. Present strength. What is it, Victor?"

"I'm about half strength, sir."

Manfield turned to the Englishmen. "That's equal to three ordinary battalions."

One of them smiled. "Even *we've* heard of the Fifty-Fifth."

"Artillery?"

"Gorman here is to give you all he's got."

"Anti-tank?"

"We're plugging your rear with twelve-pounders."

"Air support?"

"Only if strictly necessary. Probably a few Kitties."

"How long have I got?"

"A month."

It was then Kirk guessed at the things he had not been told. This attack was more important even than they had shown him. They wanted this bulge straightened out, not just to please the tidy mind of this new man Montgomery. Sooner or later it looked as though he would attack along the whole front. He was building up massively back in base areas. He would doubtless attack before Christmas, and at the full moon. That would be at the end of October. If half a battalion of Australians went west in order to prepare for a full-front attack, it was a small thing beside the entire huge conception of this war for the desert.

Then came the crowning surprise, the comic relief almost. The

Captain who had not been introduced was made known. Crowther, Counter Intelligence. "Come in, Crowther."

The Germans had agents everywhere in the cities and towns. Cairo was stiff with them. They were to be made use of. The news of the attack was to be leaked. Just the bare news, no details. For this reason, it was to be leaked by N.C.O.s or O.R.s who were utterly reliable. Only two of them. They were to be members of the Fifty-Fifth. (Realism the watchword!) The Colonel was to choose them with the utmost care.

"So," Kirk had observed. "I have also to provide two traitors."

And the whole conference had burst into laughter.

. . . . .

The rest was routine. Logistics. Map references. The mating of maps. Calculation. Method. Kirk applied himself almost fiercely. He was grateful to be all intellect for a time.

But now, up here on the sandhill, alone, he had to feel again, to admit the presence of this feeling of doom.

Perhaps it had been a mistake to put a Numerella man in charge of Numerella's Own. When a man died it was not just one less on the manning strength. It was one less in Numerella. It was not just a battalion that death had robbed. It was houses and farms, paddocks, rivers, and mountains. He knew the actual people who would get the news. He had a vision of the piece of land that man would ride no more. He knew it all: the one less joke, the one less dream, the one less drink. Numerella's Own was not its own any longer. What had claimed it, Numerella was not responsible for, did not even understand——

Bloody murder!

He stood up and called the driver:

"Time's up, Stan!"

Stan Pollock waved, took one last dive under a wave, and came running up the beach, his white buttocks looking like a pair of trunks on his dark brown body. Pollock, the Colonel remembered, was the Numerella man who drove the Council's heavy tip-truck in peace-time. His wife that slim, quiet girl who got badly burned in the bush-fires in 1938. Pollock called the Colonel "boss" when they were among their own crowd, but treated him with excruciating regimental nicety in front of strangers

"That was grouse!" he said, coming alongside the jeep and pulling shorts on over a wet body. "You should have been in it."

"Take your finger out," said the Colonel. "The whole battalion might have shot through for all we know."

"Then they can kiss good-bye to the Middle East. There'd be nothing to stop Rommel then."

As Pollock was starting up the jeep Kirk was once again glad that Ted was not in the Fifty-Fifth. The trouble was, he could never tell Freda why it was a good thing.

13

"You heard from home lately?" asked Stan Pollock.

"About ten days ago. Why?"

Kirk had answered absently, still deep in the stress of the new situation, plagued by thoughts of Freda and Ted and the new mourning to come to Numerella; but abruptly he realised the import of the driver's words.

"Why?" he repeated. "Haven't you heard?"

"Yair—that's when I last got a letter. I thought you, being the Colonel, might have heard something later, like."

"I get no privileges from the Field Post Office."

Stan devoted himself momentarily to swerving round an armoured car and then said nostalgically:

"I wonder what they're doing in Numerella tonight?"

"Much the same as any other night, I suppose," replied Kirk discouragingly.

His driver suddenly raised a chortle above the roar of the jeep's engine.

"Oh, no they won't! Tonight's Friday. Remember?"

Friday night in Numerella. Oh, yes, he remembered. He was also surprised at the power of his driver's word-portraits. There was longing in the man, for all his joviality as he reminisced.

"Just about now the pubs'll be starting to get a few in . . ."

The Railway Hotel, big, brick, and brash, pregnant with light and frilled with large cars. Not for him. Halfway down the main street the North Star was sprawling under its vine-laden roof, light coming dim, yet all the more alluringly, across the wide wooden veranda, and shining like stars between the vines that fell down in dense festoons from the roof. In the cool, still air, voices would be clear and restful, punctuated by a shout or a laugh, the voices of men and women who had done a hard day's work . . .

". . . a man rides into town, to his favourite pub, gets a beer and sits outside against a verandah post, swapping a bit of comment on this and that with the jokers nearest him. God, don't that first beer in the evenings taste good! I useter run into you in the Star quite often, usen't I? . . ."

You, and a lot of others, and some of you never again.

". . . By this time the Railway's well and truly crowded, cos the nobs have driven in to have dinner. The boys begin to drift away from the bars of the Railway, seeing the nobs'll leave their women —beg pardon, their good ladies, sipping coffee in the lounge, and come into the bars, and a man don't want to drink his beer next to a face that's been shouting orders at him all day . . ."

"I suppose," laughed the Colonel suddenly, "that's why a lot of them drifted away from the Star—they didn't want to drink their beer next to *my* face!"

Pollock merely laughed back at him. The Colonel had surprised an odd hope that Pollock might deny this.

"Down the main street," went on Stan portentously, "comes Sergeant Tolhurst, checking on each pub, to make sure that none of the boys have brought firearms into town, because sometimes when they get a bit happy they're apt to remember the last cowboy picture they saw and rush outside whooping and letting guns off into the air, and frightening Christ out of the women and kids."

"Not to mention the night the Cameron boys shot all the street lights out."

They laughed together at this memory, not Colonel and driver but two Numerella men.

"Of course," proceeded Stan, shouting above the noise of the jeep, "Sergeant Tolhurst never did like anything that went bang." Malice flashed out like a blade. "That's why the bastard joined the provosts."

"Not because he was a policeman?"

"A-a-a-a-h!" Stan hurled it into the wind. It was a sore point with a few of Kirk's men, Tolhurst joining the provosts. Privately, the Colonel thought it the only thing to do. There could have been several men in the Fifty-Fifth only too ready to pay off an old score against the Numerella police sergeant. The Colonel was tactfully quiet.

"The dance is on at the Mechanics' Institute. Bertie Rumbold's Band is beginning to warm up. Blokes are strolling along from the bars to look the sheilas over . . ."

The french chalk like a peach's down on the floor, the girls mostly in white that shone against their brown arms and shoulders, sitting in rows against the walls, handkerchiefs stuck into their bangles, chattering like lorrikeets, but the corner of an eye always on one of the lounging men, standing in assertive knots holding bottles of orangeade, in clean shirts, sharp-pressed trousers, ornate leather belts. That white enclosing their brown bodies seemed to give all women a virginal look—even women who knew intimately half the men in the town. On a soft summer's night, they were like freshly opened blooms. In the pungent grass along the bank of the river, it was like the very first time for both . . ."

Stan was remembering the river bank too:

"A lot of Numerella's necessary marriages began down on that bank."

. . . The lights of the bridge in the distance, the rumble of timbers as cars passed over it, and under the high banks the river, black, deep, and powerful, with the trees leaning over as though to breathe in its coolness.

Stan was back to comedy:

"Half past eight, and the Salvo's band's playing outside Slattery's Wine Bar, cos that's where all Numerella's worst drunks go, and you know what happens now, don't you?"

"*Poop Deck Pappy!*"

Colonel and driver roared. It was not the coast road in front of the windscreen, it was the Salvation Army Band calling forth the sinners from Slattery's Wine Bar, the worst dive in town. Sweating profusely in their thick uniforms, faces red and swollen behind their instruments which flashed in the lights, the girls prim and erect as they sang and struck their tambourines:

Shall we gather at the river?
The beautiful, the beautiful, the river?

And young men of Numerella would lean to the ears of the Salvation Army girls and whisper to them: "Shall we gather at the river?" with a totally different inflexion, and the girls, knowing what they meant, would blush, and by way of tribute the young men would join in the singing, with subversive gusto:

"Oh, shall we gather at the river?"

Out through the swinging doors of Slattery's would come the creature they called Poop Deck Pappy, product of a brief affair between a barmaid and a man who omitted to return from the First World War; bent on repenting. He was a hunched, bony man with bristly hair, a shiny scarlet face, drawn-in lips because he wore no teeth when drinking, and a great jointed beak of a nose; little eyes gleaming behind rimless glasses mended with string. The crowd would greet him with a roar. Amid the cheering and the blaring, he would take his place as if by right among the Salvos and proclaim: "I'th neen the lide!"

"Good old Poop Deck!"

The Salvos would ignore him. He was their cross, every Friday night. They couldn't deny him his repentance, even though they knew he would be back in Slattery's the very next night; they stood and sang on, played on, exhorting more fruitful transgressors, as Poop Deck proclaimed himself an unmentionable sinner, but would sin no more, had seen the light and from now on forswore the Demon Grog, only the good old Adam's Ale for him. And when the Salvos marched away Poop Deck would march away with them, swaying and staggering, gummily yelling at the sinners of Numerella to join him in the march to repentance and glory.

Colonel and driver yelled with mirth.

"He tried to join the army, you know," cried Kirk.

"Oh, Gawd!" roared Stan. "Fancy Poop Deck trying to slope arms!"

Their laughter challenged the engine of the jeep, the noise of the near-by waves.

"Hold it!" called the Colonel. "Here's our turn-off."
Just in time he had spotted the post with the battalion sign.

. . . . .

The Colonel walked into his dug-out where his Second in Command sat and announced:
"Joe, we're in strife."

14

"It stinks," said Christy at last.
"It smells sweet to me," replied Doc ecstatically. "Lovely, lovely leave!"
He coughed as the truck lurched and a dense cloud of dust came over the side. He began to laugh richly to himself.
"I know exactly what's in your mind," continued Christy. "Naked sheilas cavorting in a beery haze. Do you know what's in mine?"
"The same."
"Suspicion. Deep, dark suspicion."
"Aw, dry your bloody eyes! We're in support, the front's quiet enough for support battalions to have some leave. Pascoe put us first on the roster. Why not?"
"Not 'why not', but *why*?"
"I'll tell you," said Doc magnanimously. "Pascoe wanted a rest from you; and I'm getting leave as a consolation prize—for not being commissioned, I mean."
"You wouldn't have taken a commission."
"Pips would interfere with my freedom of action," acknowledged Doc.
"And," proceeded Christy, "they send a special truck for us, to take us back to Battalion immediately—not an order to hop the ration truck back, or find our own way, but just 'get straight aboard, leave your weapons, you're going on leave——' "
"I wonder if it'll be Cairo or Alex," Doc speculated dreamily. "Alex I want. Sister Street!"
Christy gave up in the face of Doc's glee, and was silent until the truck pulled up at Battalion Headquarters. Here, by obvious prearrangement, Sergeant Bastable awaited them. Before the tailboard of the truck was down he rasped importantly:
"Pick up your gear and follow me!"
One of the Headquarters men greeted them from a few yards away: "Aryer, Doc. Aryer, Corpus."
"No talk. Quick march," snapped Bastable. He led them straight through the hessian curtain, down the stony ramp, into the

Colonel's dug-out. Here the Colonel awaited them behind a map-strewn mess table. Bastable saluted.

"The two men you sent for, sir."

"Thanks, sarge. Who's in Battalion Headquarters beside me?"

"Only Corporal Price-Gore, sir."

"Tell him to lose himself for an hour. And for that period refer everything to the Adjutant or Major Brand. I want no man or officer in twenty yards of this *doover*. Get it?"

"Got it, sir." Bastable saluted again and withdrew.

"Stand easy, you two," began the Colonel, "and listen. Listen with your minds as well as your ears. You're going on leave to Cairo." He paused and added slowly, "A very special sort of leave. It will be the hardest thing you've ever done in the army. Harder than any action you've been in, because you're on your own and the success of an important operation that this Battalion's going to engage in depends on you. You two have been chosen because of the kind of men you are, and because I know the two of you through and through. You will be able to behave convincingly in a certain way, while holding your liquor and giving nothing away to anyone. The job will appeal to both of you, each in his own peculiar way." The Colonel allowed himself a mirthless smile. "I can see you're absolutely bewildered. Now squat yourselves on a couple of those water-tins and I'll explain. And I'm telling you in advance to wipe the grins off your faces."

. . . . .

When, fifty odd minutes later, they emerged above ground again, Doc looked awestruck and swore to himself quietly. Christy looked as though he had just been told a very subtle joke. They were waylaid by a curious Sergeant Bastable.

"Are you two villains in strife again?"

"What us?" exclaimed Doc virtuously. "We're going on leave."

Bastable gaped, then raised his head and addressed an enemy reconnaissance plane fifty thousand feet above in the heavens:

"There ain't no justice."

15

"WELL, Joe, I hope I did right," Kirk was saying to Brand.

"I think it was pretty shrewd psychology, choosing those two, Victor. They're both good soldiers, and they're both villains which means they'll play the parts to perfection."

"Did you see the look in Christy's eye as he passed you?"

"As far as I could make out, he was utterly expressionless."

"Well, I was watching him as I briefed them. Far back there was a gleam of satanic enjoyment. This was a situation after his own heart. All the farce and the mockery. Confirmation of his opinion of the human scene."

"You mean he might not take it seriously enough?"

"Oh, yes, he'll do the job to perfection. He believes in the war—in his own peculiar fashion."

"What about Doc Home?"

"First, stunned gratification at getting back among the flesh-pots, then, an absolute relish of the job he's got to do. He'll play the part to perfection—but in a different way from Christy. Doc will wallow in it. He'll love every sensual, sordid moment of it. Christy will be all sad, detached irony. There you have them—the amoral sensualist and the disillusioned moralist."

Hitherto, Major Brand had known the Colonel for what he summed up as a "good picker of men". Now he was crediting him with extraordinary insight. As a Numerella man, Kirk was not merely a good commander of "Numerella's Own"—he had begun to assume omniscient proportions. Brand's respect for him had undergone a seachange.

There was more to Diddly-Dum than caught the eye. The General had known what he was doing.

. . . . .

"Well now I've heard everything," Sergeant Bastable was saying to several Battalion Headquarters men. "That pair of rogues—the first to get leave!"

"Listen, mug," Stan Pollock told him, "they belong to a rifle company, see, and they're both bloody good soldiers, they've both just been decorated. If you're so bloody anxious to earn some leave, well transfer to one of the rifle companies and slaughter a few Huns."

"Good idea, Bastable," somebody urged. "Transfer to Don Company and give us all a holiday."

"Mind your lip!" said Bastable.

Stan Pollock told him to go and do an impossible thing.

. . . . .

Doc and Christy fended off a group of inquisitive and envious men and sought privacy, which they found, as usual, in a bomb crater. They slid down and lay against the shady slope, both looking up at the impeccable sky. For some minutes there was silence. On Doc's face was a sort of delighted wonder; on Christy's a half-smile with the beginnings of bitterness.

Doc was examining his fortune from every angle; he twisted his head this way and that as he considered: narrowed his dark slits of eyes. There had to be a catch in it somewhere. There was something Diddly-Dum had kept back. When they reported in Cairo they would get a nasty shock . . . But no! That wasn't Diddly-Dum's form.

At last he murmured reverentially:

"Well, I'll be publicly pissed on from a great height."

Christy began to laugh, quietly at first, then rose to a crescendo of dreadful, painful mirth, as Doc watched him critically. He ceased with a gulp, and stretching himself as though luxuriating, grinned and was silent, regarding the sky.

"It's affected your bloody brain," Doc commented at last.

"You're the one affected," Christy retorted. "You're positively soaked in your anticipation and your unholy delight . . . You can't or won't get beyond the fact that you've been given leave for the express purpose of dissipation. You remember the time when you've gone on leave and been warned about getting too drunk and consorting with certain women—but now you're being paid to go and do just that. You can't see the galling, farcical irony of it, can you? When—and if—we get home to Numerella, can you imagine anybody believing us if we tell them how we were once sent on leave with nice fat credits in our pay-books, with instructions to get drunk, frequent dives, and behave riotously for the purpose of betraying our country's plans to the enemy? Why it's better than anything in *The Good Soldier Schweik*. And you wonder why I'm laughing."

"Well." Doc looked uncomfortable, and shrugged it off with: "It's war, I suppose."

"That's exactly what it is," said Christy gravely. "War. Something conceived, carried out, and suffered by reasonable men, with decent instincts, fine feelings, and certain faiths. And has it ever occurred to you that situations as ludicrous as the one in which we find ourselves are taking place every day wherever the war is being fought, and all the time men, women, and kids are dying like flies, and works of art and ancient edifices are being destroyed."

"Are you quoting from something again?" asked Doc, always rendered suspicious by Christy's literary moments.

"Thank you for the implied compliment," said Christy, "but I was just expressing some thoughts provoked by the orders we've been given."

"Well, shut up," Doc told him. "I'm the senior rank here and I say this very important operation has got to be treated with complete seriousness. And you can start getting yourself in the mood for the role of a drunken bronzed Anzac thirsting for sheilas and *alicante*."

"You bloody hypocrite."

"It might be a bit funny, like, being told off to go and behave like a couple of traitors, but there's more than one way of winning a battle . . . And—well, we've got a job to do . . ."

"You self-righteous bastard."

• • • • •

They slept on their own that night, apart from the Headquarters men, turning in early, as the truck was taking them to Alexandria at daybreak.

Once, during the early hours, Doc woke from a dream of slim women and powerful drink, to roll over and murmur with the air of a dedicated man, that he was again willing to be publicly watered on from a great height.

16

Sergeant Bastable, still apparently under orders to look after them, awoke them at first light, grumpily. Doc rose like a water-spout from the sea, triumphant with the recollection of what lay ahead, and grasped Bastable, an old enemy, by his shirt:

"Thank God I don't have to look at your piggish mug for a while, or listen to your bloody repulsive voice. Give me one excuse before we shove off and I'll leave you with something to remember me by."

"You be careful," said Bastable aggrievedly.

"No," said Doc, looking the complete *bedouin*, "*you* be careful. Try not to show how crooked you are that Corpus and me are going on a well-earned leave."

Bastable, who feared them both, was obediently silent, and led them to the cook-house, where a sleepy, surly cook was also warned, or promised a swim in his own stew.

Fifteen minutes later the truck was ready for them. To their surprise, the Colonel appeared, dismissed Bastable, and had a last word before they boarded. He shook hands with both:

"I haven't come to give you a last-minute lecture. You both know what you've got to do and its importance. Good luck, and look after yourselves."

They thanked him, and he gave them a last satiric smile and told them to get aboard and not to forget to report to they-knew-where as soon as they hit Cairo.

"I'll travel in the back with you," said Doc. "I know that driver—he's a lug-punisher."

"Better tell him," said Christy.

Doc walked round to speak up at the driver's cabin; and at once there came to Christy, now aboard the truck, voices raised in disagreement, and Doc's shout:

"I'll travel where I like, and I'll be in charge from the rear!"

"Like the Duke of Plaza Toro," murmured Christy.

Doc appeared at the tailboard muttering something about 'Cheeky coots of reos."

"Climb aboard, traitor," invited Christy.

17

As the truck ran through the dawn, Christy began inwardly to exhort the landscape:

"Rise, Sun, above your bare and bloody ridges. Careful first to peer, they'll shoot at even you. Rise from pit and *sanger*, Hun, man position, clear gun. Dawn patrols return with the nightly dead. Armies, rise—rise, all, before the day is gone a lot will fall. Sweep forth, bomber, lay your awful eggs, Buzz forth, fighters, from violated hive. Gleam white, crosses, assure your carcasses below the morning dawns as ever. Prepare, O desert, for the daily racket across your barren breast! Rise, wind, swirl dust, and tanks come lumbering bear-like from your caves. All men, wise husband, good son, and caring brother, turned killer, looter, raper in your country's cause, rise and gaze through wire across the empty plain marked out for your killing ground. Rise, patriots all!"

Out loud he added: "Except you, Horrible John Jones."

"Poor old Horrible," said Doc. "I'll miss him."

. . . . .

The drive to Alexandria took two hours, for most of which they slept. Christy awoke on the outskirts of the city.

"Sing tyres on tarmac, toss O truck, and Alex welcome us, city of Greek and Jew and Levantine of wealth of sources undisclosed, of absentee landlords for whom the *fellaheen* scratch the earth with wooden stakes in Hebron Ludd and Jordan. City of ancient tales and marvellous pasts——"

"Look at that sheila there!" cried Doc. "How's that for a cute little arse?"

Knowing they would have little time in Alexandria, Doc insisted they visit a bar before reporting to Movement Control. Accordingly, they found a bar called the Cecil, hardly likely to be approved by bearers of that aristocratic name, and ordered the Egyptian behind it to open up half a dozen cold beers *iggeree.*

"Don't pour 'em, George. Just take the tops off and *shufti etneen* glasses. Don't know how to pour beer, these bastards," he confided to Christy for the thousandth time. He also believed himself to be reasonably fluent in Arabic.

"George" did as he was asked and tried to mask the gleam in his eye. He smelt money.

Doc addressed himself to his first beer as though he were commencing a rite. He held the glass beneath his nose and closed his eyes, allowing himself to breathe in the odour of hops. He took a tiny, respectful sip; then he opened his eyes wide, tipped up the glass and sent the beer down his throat in two swallows. He looked seraphic.

"Christ, that was lovely! I washed two pounds of Alamein dust down with that."

He applied himself to a second glass as "George" watched delightedly. Half an hour later, Doc, somewhat glassy of eye, rose and asked "George":

"How much *faloosh*?"

Without a flicker "George" asked an outrageous price and added a "Sir" with a winning smile. Christy cleared a couple of stools away from the bar, expecting action. Doc beamed at "George". In a mixture of English and Arabic, he informed "George" affably that he had merely ordered beer but "George" had obviously misheard him to order a bottle of something expensive. But no matter. Doc raised the flap of the counter and walking round behind the bar, helped himself to the most costly looking bottle on the shelves, which he handed across the counter to Christy. He took down another labelled "Whisky", containing liquor as dark as sarsaparilla, with a thistle-covered label that proclaimed it to be the genuine Scottish Whisky "manufactured in Glasgow Street, Scotland". This Doc rejected as "wog whisky". He was holding a tearful "George" off with one hand and reaching with the other when Christy said:

"Come on, Doc. This is vermouth. It just about cuts the bill out."

They left the bar, followed into the street by a voluble barman who was talking of provosts until Christy told him shortly that if he were to complain to the provosts about "George's" overcharging his bar would be placed out of bounds to Australian soldiers, which would no doubt render "George" *maskeen ketir*. "George" cut his losses and passed out of their lives.

They reported thence to Movement Control, where a bored officer took one look at their movement order and sprang to do its bidding. Doc winked at Christy.

"Nice to see a fogging officer waiting on you, ain't it?"

Within the hour they were on the train.

There is only one condition in which to travel on an Egyptian train. That is drunk. They are noisy, hot, smelly, and there is reason to believe that they run on saw-tooth rails and their wheels are square. All this Doc was remarking to Christy as they boarded their train. In any case, they were drunk.

18

THEIR drunkenness held a contrast in styles. Doc became selfishly, dangerously drunk: Christy quietly, drolly, and tolerantly so. At the back of his haze were always his wits.

The train they boarded was quiet enough at first. It ran with gratifying speed through the desert and the maze-like towns of hot grey mud. They sat by the window, talking idly and occasionally taking swigs from a bottle of some rich, pungent beverage. The appropriated vermouth had long since been dealt with.

By late afternoon the train was running through the Nile Valley, through the little green plots, the water-wheels, the umbrella-like palms, the small canals and the tracks where the *fellaheen* beat cruelly at monstrously laden donkeys.

The train gradually became bedlam. New and richer odours offended them as the *fellah* came aboard with his wife, his children, and his livestock. Soon the long carriage was overrun with bawling *fellaheen*, children with bare, black feet, matted hair, and eyes dim from trachoma and crawling with flies; women who huddled into their clothes and sat on large bundles; with bleating goats, screeching fowls, and baskets of fruit. Doc and Christy ensured at least elbow room by building around their seats a wall of their packs and kitbags and telling any who ventured too near to *imshi*. The *fellaheen*, cheerfulest of all downtrodden men, respected their barrier and recognising the slouch hats, began a shouted conversation in that peculiar vocabulary invented for intercourse between Arab and Australian. It consisted mostly of generous compliments or deadly insults, both of which were delivered in loud voices and in an amicable manner. The content of the remark did not matter; the act of communication was sufficient.

From their fellow travellers Christy and Doc bought, after much haggling and protestations of extreme poverty on either side, a melon and oranges. A child ran up and presented them with a hard-boiled egg and another unfolded a dirty hand to present several treacly dates, which Christy accepted with careful gravity. They toasted the *fellaheen* with their upended bottles and for the hundredth time each vowed that the other was a *quayis ketir walad*. The obscene *zigazag* was loudly exchanged with winks and leers between Doc and the men, while the women in their anonymous clothes sat with downcast eyes on their bundles. And Doc, his lesson learnt long ago in Palestine, did not so much as glance at the women; not that their aspect encouraged any gallantry.

When the carriages became choked with people and animals, new passengers getting aboard sat with their livestock along the roofs exchanging vociferous greetings or continuing with haggling begun in the village where they had climbed aboard.

With the drink numbing their brains, the noise beating at their ears, powerful alien smells pressing up their nostrils, and the sun converting the carriage into a hot-box, Doc and Christy drank even more desperately. Doc felt the need for devilry, appropriated a *fellah's* goat and insisted he wanted to buy it, as he sat back with the outraged animal on his knee. The *fellah's* entire family advanced to retrieve the goat, and Doc rose gleefully, with wicked eyes. Christy in one movement, grabbed the goat and restored it to its owners, held Doc in his seat, and reminded him what sort of a leave this was. Sulkily, Doc obeyed. He leaned back, closed his eyes, and within seconds was snoring. He had acquired that faculty so valuable to the soldier, of sleeping at will. Christy followed suit.

When they awoke it was almost dark and the *fellaheen* had all departed. Doc's pack was missing. Doc, a thief in his own right, took it without anger.

"Thieving Wog bastards," he murmured. "You'll have to lend me a spare shirt, Corpus."

"You can go and buy one," Christy told him. He never spared sympathy for the predatory Doc.

It grew quite dark, and the carriages were only lit by bulbs of spectral blue. They went back to sleep. Once in the small hours Christy woke, to see the lights like devilish orbs, that turned his thoughts, now clear, to their mission. This dark container rattling quietly through the desert night with its ghastly inward eyes was the right place, he thought, to wonder on the purpose and meaning of life. Ugh, hard-worked, unctuous phrase!

But at this moment he knew how Pascoe often felt. He was luckier than Pascoe, for he had his fortifying sense of irony; but now he felt the question enclosing him too.

Here I am travelling through the night on a mission whose purpose is to ensure that the enemy has the maximum knowledge of our plans, the result inevitably being that more of our men than necessary will be killed. No, not more than necessary. It is strictly necessary that many of us should be killed. Once the irony was missing the thought of what they were about to do was a peculiarly horrible one. For a moment he wished he could be like Doc. He wished that he could be like anyone but himself, groping in all this monstrous idiocy for some meaning, a faith of some sort . . . What had guided him so far? Experience, and the morality that experience had caused him to evolve. Or did he mean invent?

It grew light, and Doc woke to hear him murmuring:

Poor moralist, and what art thou, a solitary fly!

Doc yawned and peered out of the window from drink-bleared eyes.

"Where and what are we?"

"Egypt, the cradle of civilisation, two factors in a preposterous totient, the year 1942, humanity's second global attempt to destroy itself."

"Gawd!" marvelled Doc. "Is that what a hang-over does to you?"

19

CAIRO possessed for Christy an atmosphere that had excited him on former leaves. It seemed a place where something could happen at any time. He supposed that what created the atmosphere was the mixture of elegance and squalor, glitter and degradation, the soft purple darkness where large stars looked down on nights both Arabian and Continental. Not even tourism had ruined its features. It was a strange joy to find that the livid pictures on the parlour wall, remembered from childhood, had not been over-coloured. Not all the nonsense, pictorial and literary, which Cairo suffered had managed to make of it a disillusioning city.

The features of Cairo which counted with Doc were recognised once more. The tall, white-robed, melancholy man with the red *fez*, who paraded outside the station and announced to troops in a sepulchral voice:

"Feelthy peectures . . . feelthy peectures . . ."

Doc stopped him and looked over his wares professionally. There was nothing new in the way of pornography, and Doc shoo-ed him off. The tall man shrugged, looked distant, and drifted slowly off, tucking the revolting photographs back into his robe.

The chattering little man with oranges, calling urgently: "Oringees," and the other with the basket which held rubbery little hard-boiled eggs and loaves of bread who offered winningly: "Eggsa-bread, George? Verra nice, verra sweet, verra clean, verra hygiene."

The darting, rapid-tongued little boys who with obscene precocity offered the bodily pleasures of their sisters, which were also sweet, clean, and hygienic.

Doc brushed them aside; but then a man sidled up, dressed in a dirty white suit and with a fawning professional manner, to tell Doc that he could lead him to girls youthful, girls enthusiastic, girls medically irreproachable, girls direct from Paris.

Doc hesitated. He fingered his chin and looked appraisingly slantwise at the tempter. Christy, intervening told the man to get out of it before he called a policeman, and grasped Doc's arm.

"Your orgies have to be properly organised, remember? Try and curb your repellent lusts until we report."

Doc, looking wistful, allowed himself to be led to a *gharry*, to whose driver Christy gave an address in the Avenue Sidi Bish. "*Aywah*, George!" the driver jovially responded, and, flourishing his whip, sent the horse off at a good trot. They sat back and enjoyed the spectacle of Cairo's early morning bustle.

It was all somewhat dazzling, somewhat unreal, after their three months of life in the shell-shaken holes of the desert. No mountainous dust-fogs, or sudden, lethal rackets of gun-fire. Safety and pleasure and plenty. They blinked. It didn't matter that the sun reflected strongly on windscreens; no observers were there to summon gun-fire or strafing planes. It's like a dream, thought Christy, a fine, beckoning dream. There's a sort of wine-like newness in the air. Nothing that he observed from the *gharry* reminded him that the city of Cairo was menaced by the Afrika Corps massed in the desert not so very far away.

Beside him Doc savoured the air wolfishly. In front, the driver kept half an eye on them, for Australians had the habit of disappearing from *gharries* without paying. These two, however, dealt with him fairly.

Number 23 Avenue Sidi Bish had a blank, discreet front. A small notice alongside the door told the searcher that the British Army Special Purchasing Mission was to be found on the first floor. They climbed.

At the door which bore a twin of the notice downstairs, they knocked, and entering were confronted by an English sergeant, who asked them brusquely what they wanted, to which Doc replied Major Chapman and none of his Pommy rudeness. This exchange of courtesies brought them into an inner office and a large, quiet-spoken man in a fresh drill uniform, who was Major Chapman. He examined their documents carefully, and told them to be seated. He took from his desk a typewritten list, and holding it in front of him, began to give them their final briefing:

"This is a list of dives—and I mean dives, so you must watch yourselves—where we know that agents hang out. Alongside the name of the dive you will see the names of known agents, or the names they use. There are others whom we don't know, except by the results of their work. You will memorise this list to the satisfaction of the sergeant outside, before you leave this office. You are not to return here under any circumstances. In case of emergency, there will be a phone number for you to ring . . ."

They were told of the cheap, army-approved hotel where they would find a room, a hotel the proprietor and servants of which were known to be pro-British. The major gave them amounts of Egyptian money that made them gape. He smiled bleakly, and said as he handed it over:

"You've got to be genuinely riotous, it seems. I am told you know just how to behave."

Doc assured him this was indeed so.

The major repeated his instructions, shook hands and wished

them luck, and left them to the sergeant, who in the most regimental manner paid Doc out for his disdain by drilling their memories with ruthless thoroughness—and then beyond.

Doc was strangely docile, and Christy guessed that his friend's mind was on the delights to come. The sergeant was having a lucky escape, had he only known it; scenting the fleshpots, Doc was not quite himself, but the coming of that true self into its own lay just ahead. A resentful English sergeant was negligible. Christy felt relieved. Steering Doc through this mission was going to exhaust him soon enough. This job, in its way, was its own contradiction. Serious intentions usually called for serious methods, but in this case the method was frivolous, at least outwardly so, and was Doc's second nature. At least ten times a day, Doc, lustful and revelling, was going to forget the intention. Doc the wildcat was to do the work of the serpent and still be a wildcat. And Christy, knowing only too well what a wildcat Doc could be, was grateful for his own moral ascendancy. He was going to need it.

At last the sergeant released them. Doc's mildness had caused the sergeant to smirk, as though he were congratulating himself; but at the door Doc paused and said in a bland tone:

"Oh, Sarge . . ."

"Yes?" asked the sergeant briskly.

Doc's swift retort was so horrible that the sergeant was still silent as they closed the door.

Outside in the street, desperate men of all ages awaited them to offer food, drink, women, perversions, spectacles, and a *gharry*. Once again, Christy insisted on the *gharry*. Their hotel was about ten minutes ride away, in an alley off King Fuad Avenue. Its unlikely name was The Doncaster.

20

THE Doncaster had been meant for tourists of middle incomes in the days immediately following the building of the Suez Canal, when both British and French had impressed their character on the New City; when a tour of Egypt was part of the Grand Tour. Like Paris and Vienna, Cairo had become the setting for many a bad novel, and had suffered the same visitations. Houseboats on the Nile and the pyramids by moonlight . . . somehow, thought Christy, they were still worth having. Egypt was too ancient ever to be overtaken by phoniness.

Nowadays the front of the hotel had a scabby appearance. The pavement outside had been hosed, the sign polished, the faded tiles of the entrance scrubbed; the whole place had the cool tang of one attended to by much water; like an old shirt kept respectable by cleanliness alone.

A neat notice in the half-dark vestibule informed that it was In Bounds to All Ranks. There was a solid leather sofa flanked by large, healthy palms in earthenware pots. On the wall hung side by side an ancient coloured print of Tewfik and next to him a much newer photograph of a slim and righteous-looking Farouk, at which Doc smirked. To the Australians, the King was a smutty legend and the subject of a disrespectful song which proclaimed His Majesty to be, among other things:

King of all the wogs, all the jackals and the dogs.

Christy had previously been at much pains to dissuade Doc from singing this song in public places; and Doc had only been convinced of its offensiveness when an Egyptian Army officer had drawn his sword on Doc one night at a cinema. That had been in 1941 when the Fifty-Fifth had come out of Tobruk, and Doc and Christy had found themselves on the same leave party in Cairo. Since the King was reputedly unsympathetic to the Allied cause, officers encouraged rather than condemned such chauvinism as Doc loved to indulge in. Christy had once or twice thought how much simpler life was to somebody so utterly insensible to the emotions of others, as Doc. Doc could cheerfully insult anything on God's earth, from a person's dearest faiths to a nation's most sacred institutions.

Behind the reception desk sat a large, flabby woman whose breasts met her waist-fat. She wore a black dress and smiled with a sallow, handsome face as their boots rang on the tiled floor. She deferred her gaze to Doc's stripes, and Doc, leaning on the desk, asked:

"You speak English, Mum?"

Still smiling, she inclined her head and replied in a tuneful voice:

"I speak very well English, gentlemen."

"Good on yer," applauded Doc. "Well, we want a nice, clean room, see?"

"We have very nice and clean rooms. Please, gentlemen, you and friend must show me your leave pass. It is the provost regulation."

Having inspected their leave passes, she excused herself and went down a passage to the back regions, whence presently came her own and another voice speaking rapidly in Arabic. She came labouring back in a few minutes, in slippered feet and on swollen legs, followed by a skinny girl also in a black dress and with a small white apron. In build, she was adolescent, but the alert and petulant face was that of a woman of thirty. Still some yards away from them, she said rapidly: "I will show you room, very clean. Upstairs. Please follow."

They obeyed. As they mounted the staircase she still chattered:

"You have seen notice of charges? Fixed by army, boys, you

pay one week in front. If you like drink, we have bar next door, or Ibrahim will bring, you just call down stairs "Ibrahim!" You can bring girls, but no noise and not drunk, and not in daytime, boys, because we must clean——"

Doc put an arm round her boyish waist and she looked at him with a swift sideways flash of her pretty, dark eyes, and giggled perfunctorily.

"How about if I want girl in daytime? You?"

He patted her behind, and something of his lustful tension went into her like a small shock. Plainly roused, she let his hand stay at her buttocks, and gave him a managing smile:

"You Aussies bad boys, but very nice. I am respectable girl, Sergeant."

"And I'm a respectable boy," Doc assured her. "Ask me mate here."

Christy sighed. "Aren't you tired after all that grog and the trip? Can't you wait, you randy bloody animal?"

"I've got to get the dirty water off me chest straight away," Doc told him earnestly. "Don't worry, I haven't forgotten," he added significantly.

Christy turned to the woman, now looking proprietorially at Doc:

"We'll have separate rooms, I think, Esmeralda. Lead on. I want some sleep."

She led them to the first room, silent now, and opened the door for Christy. He turned to Doc:

"I'll see you at sunset, when its cooled off, and we'll go out. I hope you have some energy left."

Doc winked, and crooning to the woman, on whose hips he now had an unshakable grip, he went on and left Christy to his rest. She'll take him for a few quid, thought Christy as he closed his door. She's got a hard, financial look in those eyes. And serve him right.

The room, which had a tiled floor, lime-green walls, and large french windows hung with clean lace curtains, contained a wall cupboard, a commode, and an ornate old iron bedstead, on which he immediately collapsed, to slumber dreamlessly.

When he awoke it was early evening. The sun coming in the windows was cool and dim, and outside he could hear the restful sounds of the day's end. Men in a café across the street sat slackly and talked without tension in their voices; for good or ill, success or failure, the actions of the day were done, life one day less young, night could bring its balm and its small adventures. Christy rose and looked outside. In the sandy garden below two Arab boys sat playing with small coloured cards beneath a palm. Behind reared the moss-grown roundness of a dome and slender minaret that pointed as though to draw attention to the glowing sunset.

The world seemed to be listening to itself, to catch its own echoes.

Your mood was so often a matter of time of day. If it could only be always *this* time of the day, and this mood! Perhaps it could solve problems of hate, passion and striving; soothe ambition, soften the edges of rivalry. Nonsense! In similar sunsets he had shot men and seen others die.

His door opened, and Doc came in clad in nothing but a towel, his hair dripping.

"How're you feeling, Corpus? I found a bathroom down the passage, shower, and the lot. I've just had a dip."

Christy scowled at him:

"Did she wash your back for you?"

21

"I HATE to sound like a nag." said Christy, "but I feel it my duty to remind you that we must be dissolute in an organised fashion."

Though he spoke with a dryness appropriate to the words, there was yet in his tone an intense savour of them, and Doc, discerning that Christy was enjoying the situation in a sense that he himself could not understand, did not resent them. Lazily and benignly, he surveyed the passers-by.

"I might feel it my duty to remind you that I'm the senior rank in this contingent," he said with half-shut eyes. "I can be dissolute, as you call a bit of fun, in an organised fashion, a disorganised fashion, and any old way you like. I'll serve every non-syphilitic sheila in Cairo, drink every bottle of beer they care to put on the ice for me, and carry out our, er, mission to the satisfaction of the General Staff."

They were sitting at an open-air table outside a restaurant, sipping cool lagers. It was called the Restaurant de l'Est, and Christy knew it to have good food. They have already inspected the menu and Christy had settled on clear soup, *cote de veau* with green salad, French pastry and a bottle of whatever white wine they could drag up. Doc, to whom good food meant nothing more than steak, eggs, and chips, had ordered accordingly.

The evening crowds were drifting by, colourful, like fallen fragments of the sunset: Egyptian, Greek, Levantine, French, and Jew, with British uniforms scattered among them as sober reminders of what lay westward.

"Look at 'em," mused Doc. "If Rommel takes Cairo, they'll come out with flags and hail him as a liberator."

"The Jews won't," Christy told him. "Remember all the cyklon gas we found in that dump near West Point 27? I'll bet that was for those poor devils."

"Do you reckon it's true, all this about what Hitler's supposed to be doing in Germany, and elsewhere?"

"Remember those refugees that came over the Syrian border? You heard the things they said the same as I did."

"What'll they do to the Aussies? We've treated 'em pretty rough. I haven't taken a prisoner since one night at Tobruk, when they wanted a Jerry for questioning."

"They respect us. We're realists. Half the time, when we do a stink, we can't spare the men to take prisoners back—so we shoot them. They understand that. They think we're like them—only we're not. We know how to laugh."

"What'll the Jerries do after the war—after we've won, I mean?"

"What makes you think we'll win?"

"You think we'll lose?"

"H'm. There are more ways than one of losing a war. The trouble with wars is that the moment the last shot has been fired, the heroes become ineffective."

"That another of your famous quotes?"

"No, but I can give you one. Even you have heard of Lawrence?"

"The joker in A Company who got the V.C.?"

"Lawrence of Arabia."

"Oh, yair. Led the wogs against the Turks in the first war, and got sold down the river."

"He wrote of how they lived many lives in their whirling campaigns, wrought up with ideas inexpressible and vaporous, but to be fought for. But when they had triumphed and the new world dawned, the old men came out to re-make the world in the likeness of the former world they knew . . . *We stammered we had worked for a new heaven and a new earth and they thanked us kindly and made their peace*."

"Silly bastard," grunted Doc.

"And yet you knew he was 'sold down the river'. You surely haven't read *The Seven Pillars of Wisdom*?"

"The only book I've read in years is *Maria Monk*. No, I heard you and Roy Pascoe quoting it to each other one day, back in Beit Jerja."

The waiter came with the clear soup, which Christy found distinctly oniony

"Here, George," Doc offensively addressed the French waiter, "where's my bull's bum? You sent down to the abattoirs for it?"

The man gave him a nervous, uncomprehending smile, and hurried away on Christy's reassurance.

"Sometimes I wonder why you ever joined the bloody army," ruminated Doc. "You didn't join just for the adventure like me, you're too much of a ratbag. Why the hell *did* you?"

"Sometimes I wonder myself. Like most other decisions, or gestures, it was a combination of circumstances. The men I liked and respected most joined up: Vic Kirk, Joe Brand, Roy Pascoe, Charlie Mann. Whatever our own sins, Fascism was a gigantic going-backwards. It was against every instinct that ever prompted any good act of mine. Whatever the betrayals subsequent to victory, they would be preferable to the Fascist alternative."

"You're too bloody complicated for me," Doc told him. "I remember you making pacifist speeches in the pub at home."

"Not pacifist—anti-war."

"What's the difference?"

"You never knew my father, of course."

"Only as a tree in the Avenue of Honour."

"My father's tree was a later addition. He did not die till some years after the war, having spent those years in the Repatriation Hospital at Brisbane in a bath of oil, half the flesh gone from his body. He could have been accurately described as a piece of partly-cooked meat. I was at the reputedly most impressionable age in the years when I visited him, before he finally gave up his half-life, long overdue, to death. I used to face him with pity and protest held tight at the back of my throat, like a bitter acid ball. Like something embalmed he looked, all ready for the bindings. His face was a curious lilac shade with deep black lines that had nothing to do with age; they were put there at once, with pain and fear and horror, like so many quick strokes of a knife. His eyes seemed to grow out of his face like two shiny *fungi*. There was nothing else in it. Pity leaves you after a time, in such cases. There is little left but horror or revulsion. The legless soldier can be admired or pitied. Of course, the most convenient kind is the dead one. He is not there to make inconvenient demands as a price for his sacrifices. No promises made to him to be kept. He is always good for a speech or two, memorials, ceremonies, and the rest, provide numerous opportunities for gathering prestige and exploiting public emotion. But men like my father are shut well away, like terrible family secrets in a closed wing of a house. The only thing that could give him dignity was death and death held off playfully for some time, like a cat delaying the end of a mouse——"

Doc shuddered, and closed his eyes fully. In the darkness of his lids an image began to grow like a distant smear of light; something thrust at him in the blackness, faintly hurtful, something of a life he had once entered so very briefly, so very long ago, he had forgotten to identify himself with it any more. But it was there: the tiny echo of a hurt, the ghost of a gleam from a time well lost.

He opened his eyes again and looked at Christy who, his soup finished, was once more gazing at the passers-by. He saw as if for the first time Christy's sensitively-boned features with the uncomfortable blue eyes, the tight, wide, sardonic mouth, the coarse, grey-streaked hair. Emotion in Doc became wholly identifiable. He spoke gruffly:

"You want to put things like that out of your mind, mate. Life's too short to brood about anything or anybody. Eat, drink, and be merry, tomorrow we foggin' well die—that's the only quotation I ever learned. And die we bloody well may! So who cares? Why be bitter? We've all got something in the past we could dwell on. Put it down to experience. Fog 'em all!"

"You!" said Christy harshly. "You fifth-rate bacchanalian, what have you got in your past that you need be bitter over?"

Doc looked at him resentfully. He shrugged, as if to rid himself of something. The thing felt was still there. He had uttered his brief, second-hand philosophy as much for his own benefit as Christy's, but it had not had its effect. For the first time, Christy's contempt had struck home, and he wanted to justify himself.

"I'm not saying I've had your experiences. I'm a lot smarter than you, mug. Well, yer see . . . Look, I was going on the square with a sheila once. I won't say I did me balls on her—but I *was* on the square." Doc looked so unlike Doc as he made this emphasis that Christy was strangely disturbed. "It was Toowoomba. I was seventeen I think. I met this sheila at the show—I was there selling fairy floss at a tray a shot and touching the odd mug when I could find him. She was working in a sideshow. Billed as the Snake Woman, she was. Used to fool round with tiger-snakes and red-bellies, with their poison sacs and their fangs out, of course. She used to stand up there with just a pair of shorts and a brassière covered in spangle things and let these snakes coil all over her. I got into the way of going in the tent to watch her whenever I could. Got a queer sort of a kick watching those snakes on that nice white flesh. Cold like. Used to imagine the snake was me—or a part of me. Well, there was a pimply fat piece in a milk bar I used to manage to have as long as I didn't look at her face . . . but by this time it was this snake sheila or nobody.

"Well, she noticed me in the end—couldn't help it, I suppose, and woke up to what I was after. First time we spoke she turned it on—I was like a rat up a rope! She was twenty-six, but I was big for me age, and I didn't need no instruction from her, even then.

"It looked like we were good for each other. We started to go steady. I got her to leave the snake caper, because I wouldn't have other jokers staring at her without clothes. We got two rooms in the back of a house and set up together. We swore we were going to get married as soon as we had enough dough. I worked at about four different lurks; sold the fairy floss, tic-tacked at the races, bought old pies at the factory, hotted them up and sold them at the footie on Saturdees. Even did a couple of burglaries.

"She got a job doing housework at a big house up near Webb Park. Used to come home still wearing her black dress, and for some reason that tight black dress always got me worked up. She was a big beefy blonde and waggled her hips like two water-melons in a sack. Her name was Olive—Olive Tremayne . . . Only it wasn't. Her real name was Thelma Hopkins. She couldn't even tell the truth about that. And there was no job at no big house. She was on the game. The dough she pretended to be wages was something else. One of her customers was the bloke who ran the side-show with the snakes—but she was the biggest snake he ever captured. A high-class rut, she was, and she was still going to marry me. When I faced her with it she just said, So what, we can still go on as before, these jokers don't mean nothing to me, and look at the dough. I might turn it on for them, but you're the only one I'd sleep with——

"I knocked her cold, and kicked her arse as she lay there. Then I went round to the sideshows and nearly killed that bloke.

"When I told the coppers about it, they finally broke down the charges, but I still did six months . . ."

Doc paused musingly:

"Thelma Hopkins taught me everything I needed to learn about sheilas, their characters and their uses. It don't matter how low they are, they like to have a bloke's name—they like people to call them Missus. Until I met Thelma, I always thought that sheilas had to be talked into a bit of a naughty. But they want it as bad as us.

"The sheilas I've promised to marry as long as they gave in! The sheilas that have fallen for a bit of soft soap or a few grogs under their pinnies!"

Doc ended. He looked all *bedouin*, white teeth smiling as predatory as a shark's, black eyes gleaming, light all along his sharp, curving nose, as he turned to Christy.

"Fog 'em all! Enjoy yourself, that's what the Doc says."

A big, beefy, blonde, thought Christy. But now it was all thin, frail brunettes. There was a moral there, in an immoral way. He imagined Doc's sole, brief groping after respectable, established, recognised things. The attractive wife, the steady income, the right to be called Mister. Respect accorded you because of your virtue and not the danger you implied.

Could Doc be termed a typical child of the Depression? He had undoubtedly left school long before he should, at seventeen he probably behaved like, and was thought of as, twenty-seven. What was the instinct that had made him seek respectability with the sluttish Olive Tremayne? An overlaid one? Yes! Doc's natural instincts were explicit today. He was a certain kind of a man, who reacted instead of reflected, who wanted only one lesson, for it was enough for Doc to judge the whole by the part. Just for once, at seventeen, he had failed to see with clear eyes, for they had been clouded by an uncharacteristic yearning—never to be repeated. Olive Tremayne—what a name!—had confirmed for him the kind of man he was. And done him a favour. Doc saw that now. He had no pity for himself. He despised Christy for risking more punishment. After his father, that should have been Christy's lesson: let some other mug join the army and get mangled. Yet in Doc's story, in his one, fruitless, vulnerable stumble into morality Christy saw something inexplicably pathetic.

"That soup," said Christy, "was like camel piss. Its upset my guts."

"Feeling crook?" asked Doc.

"No, humbled. We are each his own prisoner."

. . . . .

Their food came, and they applied themselves to it for the next fifteen minutes. The *cote de veau* was excellent, and Doc spoke well of his rump steak.

"Which of these joints do we visit first?" he asked Christy when they had finished. "You know Cairo better than me."

"There's a place not far from here that's on our list. The Halcyon."

"The Halcyon," echoed Doc. "Don't know it."

"It's a Greek word. It implies pleasure."

"Now you're talking," said Doc. "Lead on, Corpus."

22

THE Halcyon was a basement of a large building and looked as if it had been an expensive restaurant about forty or fifty years ago. Its panelled walls were darkened by time and smoke. Upon these walls some not very talented artist had painted larger-than-life figures of nude women. It was divided into booths, given privacy by potted palms and bead curtains. There was a long bar at the far end as they entered, and lurid modernity was represented by lights behind long panels of coloured glass. Large, old fans swished softly from a low ceiling. From somewhere a radio gave forth whining Moorish music. The women who sat around in bored pairs or competently egging an odd British soldier on to drunkenness while they sipped soda water that they called gin, were a cheap, worked-out-looking lot. They had obviously been a long time in their game and didn't expect to get any further. Next stop was the brothel or the room in the *burqa*. One or two glanced sharply and hopefully at the two newcomers, and preened their false finery.

"Look at 'em," chuckled Doc. "Ever noticed when a sheila's getting ready for the fray, she smooths the front of her dress and sticks out her tits?"

With mock dignity Christy retorted:

"I need no instruction in the erotic significance of the mammiform."

"Come again!"

"Oh, shut up—we are now on duty."

"So we are, bejeesus! Bloody fantastic, ain't it?"

As they reached the bottom of the short stairway, Doc asked:

"Who's the suspect here?"

"A Greek called Stavros."

"That's right, a dago."

Doc's illusions were all of a social or racial kind. The British, and the Australians in particular, were of a superior mould. Arabs (wogs), Jews (five-to-two's), Greeks (dagoes) were all lesser races under the sun, and not a serious proposition. They found a booth and sat down. In a few moments a woman had joined them.

She was a plump creature with lank hair who wore her dress like an extra skin. It was a scarlet dress with huge yellow flowers on it, cut so low in front that it looked as though her nipples must at any moment be perspiringly bared. She shook her barrel-like hips, flung a string of heavy beads over her shoulder, and asked them with the calm air of the specialist:

"Come for a good time, boys?"

Doc eyed her without favour:

"No, we thought this was a church."

She gave a shrill chortle, grating in its insincerity, and said in an accent meant to be either Australian or American:

"Say, that's bloody good! Eh?"

Deftly, she entered and sat herself within the booth.

"That's what I like about you Aussie boys—so humorous. I bet you won't say no to a drink—like hell!"

"We'll have two cold beers, and mind they're cold," Doc said. "If you get cold ones you have one yourself."

She rose. "I'll have gin, big boy."

"You'll have beer, big girl. I'm not paying gin prices for lemonade." He eyed her through shining slits of eyes, and added: "Like hell."

She pouted with lips that shone like bloody meat and moved off, throwing her hips about heftily for their benefit.

Doc sighed. "The things I do for my country!"

"What's wrong with her?" asked Christy. "She's doing her best."

"For one thing," Doc told him, "she's cornered the body-odour market."

"Throw a bottle of scent over her before you drag her into bed."

"What makes you think I'd drag *her* into bed?" Doc expostulated. "Why——"

"I've seen you make advances to worse than her," Christy told him unsympathetically. "Besides, she might be what we want."

"Then *you* drag her off," cried Doc triumphantly. "I order you to."

"I don't think she's anything but what she seems," said Christy. 'Just some poor slut earning an undignified living."

"If you're so bloody sorry for her take her home tonight and let her earn a few quid."

The subject of their conversation returned, with another girl, whom she presented, as though on approval, to Christy. She was a tall, dark girl, wide-shouldered and deep-chested, who carried her back with a rearing dignity. She sat down quietly, and looked unsmilingly in front of her. She had the raven hair, worn in a bun, and the straight nose of the Greek. Her large fine eyes held a proud glitter, a glitter which could have been the held-in fire of contempt, for she was clearly in strange waters, and the first girl spoke to her in the way of the tutor, the prompter.

Her name was Kozeta, her mentor told Christy, and then introduced herself as Sophie. Christy caught the attention of a wandering waiter and ordered more drinks. Kozeta took hers up slowly, still looking ahead, sipping it as a patient might sip some necessary potion, erect and silent in the pride of some habitude she had lost. To her new territory, her point of descent, she was paying tribute by her presence alone. Sooner or later, thought Christy, the step would come. The drunken soldier to be prompted and flattered into buying drinks; the thick, sodden, confidential voice that said he wanted to come home with her; the walk back through the darkness, the opening of her door, the man making free of the room, of her bed, of her: the first fee-paid invasion of man as flesh alone with a lust to be freed of.

He broke in on his own thoughts, as though he had caught himself out in some evasion, some lapse of intellect. He felt inclined to laugh at himself. What did you call a man who got sentimentally concerned over a prostitute? Each had her beginnings. There had no doubt been a time when the over-ripe, professional Sophie had felt a strange man between her thighs and held revulsion inward. He supposed he had better start getting lewd with this Kozeta, mauling her, and not in any consoling way, or she might break down and try to give him her life story, or see him as a deliverer; which latter, in view of his purpose in being here at all, would be too sardonic even for him.

So he put an arm around her and drew her roughly closer. She responded by a slight movement.

"You're Greek, aren't you?"

She smiled a little, as though the word "Greek" warmed her with the sense of better things, and nodded. Gravely, she asked:

"Many Australians fought in Greece. You were there?"

"Yes," he lied. I can brazen it out, he thought. I've listened to enough Australians who were.

"Which part of Greece?" she asked, twirling her glass between her fingers, carefully, as though the very question held its own dangers.

"Well, many parts. We were in retreat, you know, Germans chasing us, and we did not know where we were most of the time."

"Then," she stated with calm simplicity, "you fought at Thermopylae."

"Oh, yes!"

Strange fate for a legendary name, he thought. The Pass, whose name stood for perhaps the most illustrious battle in history, a name to which Australians had added a short, tragic stamp of their own as the bulk of their army fled south, now being glibly lied about in a dive, to an apprentice prostitute, for a shoddy, devious end.

She looked at Christy directly for the first time and said with a pride that was now naked and challenging:

"My brothers die there, too."

Enough! He downed his beer recklessly. It was another Greek they were after. He affected a slurred tone and shouted at Doc:

"Hear that, mate? This girl's brothers died at Thermopylae. I was telling her we were there—how we liked the Greeks."

"Cripes, yes!" Doc agreed largely. He snapped his fingers and looked impatient. "Last time we were in Cairo, we came in here and drank with a very nice Greek man. What was his name? Star——Stav——something . . . Oh, what was it?"

"Stavros?" prompted Kozeta.

"That's it! Stavros! Does he still come here?"

"Stavros is gone," said Sophie shrugging. "He was arrested."

"You don't say! Poor old Stavros! What for?"

Sophie shrugged again:

"Who knows? He was in all kinds of bad things. He tried to get the girls here to take drugs at his flat."

"He was a bad Greek," said Kozeta, as though to be bad as a Greek was the worst type of all badness, the worst of all betrayals, since to be Greek was the best of all things.

Doc and Christy ordered more drinks; the girls were allowed gin on condition that it really was gin, to which they agreed. Sophie drew forth a bottle of scent and sponged as much of her bosom as the dress revealed with it, then let a few drops fall down between her breasts. This, and the drink, seemed to excite Doc, and he became more kindly disposed towards her. It was obvious to Christy that beneath the table he had his hand up Sophie's dress. It was worth staying in the place, thought Christy. A few more beers and they would let out some "drunken" secrets.

He drew Kozeta closer and told her she was beautiful; he had not seen her there the last time he had visited the place. She put up her chin and said defensively:

"I came only two days ago. I get away from Salonika in a boat and reach Alexandria. I come here and meet Sophie. One day," she added with pathetic hardiness, "I find good job."

(Like hell you will! You have no papers. If the British get you they'll stick you in a camp of some sort, and you'll get even shorter shrift from the Egyptians. It is barely possible that this Stavros was blackmailing you into picking up information. Look as tragically proud as you like, my girl, hug the memory of your brothers to you like a medallion warm to your breast, but, blameworthy or not, you could, through your circumstances, be on the other side. I'm going to spill something, just to be on the safe side.)

As if he had actually spoken aloud to her, he grasped her knee hard as if to commiserate with her for harsh words. She grasped his hand in response and said with a sudden, audacious air of committal:

"You want to stay with me tonight?"

He nodded and toasted her silently and unsteadily. She smiled as if relieved.

Suddenly he was tired and very bitter. (It might be all an act. It might be some clever way of getting a good payment through sympathy from certain sorts of mug—like himself.) His beer was transformed into the stuff of life and was nauseous on the tongue.

Doc, now hot and deep in prurience, was asking Sophie if there was a room in the place where he could take her. She was admitting in urgent whispers that there was—"special place"—but wouldn't later be better—"more time for love?" Couldn't the big bronze Anzac wait, was he so passionate for his Sophie? With his lust abated, Doc might be less inclined to continue drinking, and the drinks did mean commission for her, which meant more than mere commission, since she needed to induce the ordering of sufficient drink to be allowed in the place, and so remain to sell herself after hours, and not on commission. Thus Christy read her thoughts.

Doc, ever to the point, offered her a fair sum of money. Presently, they went away behind some bead curtains in an obscure corner. A white-coated waiter smirked tiredly as they disappeared, Sophie's buttocks heaving exultantly as the beads swung back on them.

Well, Doc would spill himself to Sophie. Christy turned back to Kozeta. He urged more drink on her and drank more himself. He began in reality to become a little drunk. He patted her hand:

"I will pay the Germans back for your brothers. Soon. Next month. The first two Germans I shoot I will shoot for you."

She grasped his hand with sudden, honest force.

"I would like to go with you now. Your friend will stay with Sophie."

He looked at his watch. It was eleven o'clock. Late enough.

"Come to my hotel," he said.

She nodded. "I will go out first, and wait. You come in a few minutes."

She rose, and walked very straight and quick from the Halcyon.

He watched her disappear, and sat back thoughtfully. Was this the very first time for her in reality? There was this proud delicacy, asking him to follow her outside in a few minutes. She did not want anybody in this place to know of their assignation by seeing them leave together . . . Well, if it were the first time, why not with him? Perhaps he could see himself as some kind of lesser evil.

. . . . .

She stood in the shadow just near the entrance. She took his arm. She looked big, straight, and handsome as she walked beside him. She did not speak. He felt almost connubial.

At the hotel, she walked past the flabby woman at the desk without looking at her, and mounted the stairs regally.

In the room, Christy closed the door and turned to find her standing looking at him. Her expression was hard to read, but there seemed to be respect for him in her regard. Then, almost defiantly, she undid the front of her dress.

She was slow to find passion at first; but suddenly it was as if he had touched a hidden spring; she said something hoarse in her own language, and responded to him strongly. At the climax, she uttered a deep low cry of repletion and spoke rapidly in her own language once more.

Some minutes later as he lay listening to her deep, slow breathing, he touched the bare shoulder and said:

"Listen, on the fourth of next month at El Alamein, my battalion, the Fifty-Fifth, is going to attack the Germans. The first two Germans I shoot, I will say 'That is for the brothers of Kozeta.' I promise."

She turned, kissed him gently, and whispered:

"And the third for Kozeta."

False, malicious, distrustful state of all things! Even as he felt his intense liking for her, he told himself that if she was a fraud and an informer his promise would have fulfilled a duty; if she was what she seemed to be, the first three—supposing he got them—would indeed be for Kozeta and the brothers of Kozeta.

The brothers of Kozeta. It sounded like the title of a poem. He might write just such a poem, but not for some time yet. It was his last waking thought.

In the dead hours he awoke and found she was gone.

23

Doc, wet from the shower and fresh as ever, entered his room and woke him at half past ten. Sun came through the french windows, the world hummed, clashed, and haggled without. Doc carried a bottle of beer, which he upended and drank from. He had a theory, from heaven knew where, that if you took the top from a bottle of beer, let it stand overnight and drank it flat first thing in the morning, hang-over never visited you.

"Where's Cosy—whatshername?"

"Safe in her own bed, I trust. Where's your pocket battleship?"

"I gave her the shove at the Halcyon. I acted drunk and started skiting about what we were going to do to the Jerries on the fourth of next month. She told me she wasn't interested in the war. Didn't look it either. She performs as if it's going to be her very last. How did you go?"

"Much the same. I said I was going to shoot a couple of Huns for her brothers on the fourth of next month."

"She was a sulky piece, wasn't she? How was that act? Hard to get, I'm not used to this sort of thing, oh-my-poor-brothers. I suppose it gets a few in . . ."

"What makes you certain it was an act?"

"Course it was! All crows have their little stories of the tragedy that turned 'em into a crow. Don't I know it! I bet you at this very moment Thelma's telling some mug she's sleeping with for the night about the bloke that done her wrong."

Christy had a mordant envy of Doc at that moment, for his unreflecting certitude of mind. Correct or incorrect, it was a comfortable way to be. He supposed he himself would always be the same: the questionings, the search in the dense mass for the ore of goodness or honesty. No doubt a romantic prospecting.

He rose from the bed. "What's the programme?"

Doc pointed to the bed:

'She left you a souvenir."

On the sheet lay a thin gold ring. She had worn such rings in her ears, Christy recalled; this ring must have been torn from an ear; if he remembered, they were pierced. Painful.

"Yair," he agreed, and picked it up.

There was a knock at the door and he hastily threw a towel around his bare body and called out "Come in!" The flabby woman, who seemed to have taken an implicit fancy to them, entered with a tray carrying coffee, bread, dates, and a flower in a tooth-glass. She smiled at them, and looked more handsome than ever.

Christy thanked her warmly, for the tray had not been asked for.

Without speaking she dipped her dark head at them, and left, labouring on her swollen legs.

Doc chuckled:

"She's got an eye on you."

"You evil-minded bastard, haven't you ever heard of a disinterested act?"

"The lure, mate! The lure!"

"Oh, shut up!" said Christy crossly.

. . . . .

"I want a proper breakfast," Doc grumbled half an hour later. "Steak and eggs. Come on!"

Christy, shuddering, followed him from the hotel, into the alley, and thence into the gaudy bustle of King Fuad Avenue.

He watched fascinated while, in a small café, Doc put away a huge helping of steak and eggs. Doc was never in danger of becoming alcoholic: drink made him hungry for food, as well as other things.

"Well," asked Doc, making a last, satisfied swallow, "how do you reckon we went last night?"

"Only so-so. I don't think either of them was interested in picking up info from soldiers. Still, they might repeat what we told them in the right quarter. I think we should assume we missed out at the Halcyon."

"Yair . . . probably this Stavros being run in has sort of put an end to things for a bit. I bet Sophie knew what he was up to. There's no flies on *her*."

A dark-skinned man in a grubby light suit approached, cringing and hopeful.

"Fog off?" Doc told him, picking his teeth. "Hey, Corpus, how about a swim?"

"Good idea!" agreed Christy. "We can go along to Sednaoui's, buy a couple of pairs of trunks, and spend the morning making ourselves wet inside and out."

"Come on," Doc said, rising. He raised a hand to a passing *gharry*:

"Hey, George! Woa back!"

"George" obliged, and they climbed aboard.

"Where can we swim?" Doc asked.

"There's a good pool at Gezira. But we'd better take a taxi—it's a fair way."

Leaving Sednaoui's, where Doc was surprised at its size and efficiency—run by Wogs!—they got a taxi and told the driver to take them to Gezira. Doc settled back contentedly.

"You ever been out to the pyramids?" Christy asked him.

"Fog the pyramids."

"Or Memphis and Sakhara?"

"Fog 'em!"

"Or the Valley of the Kings?"

"Fog the kings! And fog the queens too!"

"Listen, you animal, they're sights worth seeing. People travel across the world for that very purpose."

"The only scenery I'm interested in is what's underneath a dress."

Christy sighed and gave up.

They spent till the early afternoon at Gezira, wetting themselves, as Christy had proposed, inside and out. On their way back, Christy re-introduced the subject of sightseeing, but found Doc, even with a fair amount of beer aboard, still unresponsive.

"You keep your mind on the job," he told Christy virtuously. "We didn't come here to waste the army's time gaping at ruins."

. . . . .

That night they visited a large cabaret called the Bardia: a gleaming, gaudy, echoing place, with an upstairs balcony round all four walls from where they could look down on a four-piece band, a hundred crowded tables, and a smoke-wreathed, drink-released crowd of servicemen who sat with women of several, and some unguessable, nationalities. It was a "modern" place; that is, wherever metal was used it shone with chrome, the lighting was all behind glass, and the furnishings were all angular and ugly. It was a fairly expensive place, and for this reason was In Bounds to Sergeants and Above. Christy had borrowed a set of Doc's stripes to wear for the occasion. Doc had proposed the Bardia as the next on their list because it was famous for its belly-dancers, and he was fascinated by them. Soon enough, one of them appeared and Doc sat back with the air of a connoisseur.

She was an Algerian girl with eyes heavily outlined in black like a Matisse painting, and hung with glittering jewellery. The upper part of her brown body was bare, to show pear-shaped breasts and a belly whose size could have been that of about seven months' pregnancy; which Doc affirmed until Christy told him that she was a professional who cultivated a belly for the sake of her "art". A skirt was strung two inches below the navel.

She began to dance, slowly at first, to the whining music, the monstrous tummy circulating, undulating, rolling, and shivering as the voices of men urged her to more frantic efforts. As the speed of the music increased, so did the antics of the gleaming brown belly, and the hoarse approval of men turned into delighted shouts and shrill whistling. The music became phrenetic, hysterical, and the belly resembled an eccentric wheel whose hub was the navel. She turned slowly as she danced to display her quivering buttocks, and win a cry of ecstasy from the avid Doc. Her upraised face was rapt, sweating, and enigmatic, her arms flung straight above her head; her jewellery tinkled rhythmically. Finally, with a scream the music ceased; she dropped her arms and the belly became almost miraculously motionless. To a clamour of applause and lewd shouts she ran out behind a curtain.

A British sergeant rose to follow her. A naval petty officer rose and felled him. He was grabbed from behind by another sergeant whom he tossed over his shoulder on to a table, which collapsed on top of a girl who began to scream like a mad thing. The petty officer was hit with a bottle, and sank with a bloody head. A flying-officer picked up a vase of flowers and broke it over the closest head, which happened to be that of a naval man. This being a clear declaration of alliance, each naval man promptly turned violently upon the nearest enemy, army or air force. Doc rose, the unholy light of battle in his eyes. Unfortunately, there were no naval men on the nearly empty balcony. He had to make do with an under-sized flight-sergeant, who, after dodging one wild, homicidal swing, scuttled exclaiming down the back stairs. Doc, eyes roaming for new engagements, found himself grabbed from behind by Christy. A knee jammed cruelly into the small of his back.

"Any nonsense from you," said Christy's voice, "and I'll ruin your kidneys."

"It's a barney," Doc expostulated. "What do you expect a man to do?"

"Ordinarily, I wouldn't give damn what happened to you——"

"Provosts!" came the cry from the *melee* below, and men in uniform ceased their fighting, hugged each other in sentimental armistice, to turn upon the common enemy—the Provost Corps.

"Aw, let's get out of it," said Doc. "They're all Pommies anyway. It's not our fight."

"Not so easy now," Christy told him.

Down below them the wreckage-strewn floor was aswarm with the red caps of British provosts.

"They'll have the joint plugged at every door," said Christy. "And you know how these bloody red-caps hate Aussies. They'll grab us with the greatest of good will."

Doc grabbed up a table after tipping a girl out of her chair to do so.

"Let's bomb a few of the bastards."

He carried the table to the railing and poised it there. A pair of red-caps came into view, pushing a bleeding petty officer between them. Casually, Doc released the table. There was a crash and a cry of anguish from below.

"I hope you hit the coppers," said Christy, "and not the poor bloody matelot."

Doc peered cautiously over. "I did," he gloated.

"Then let's scarpa," Christy told him. "There's a balcony behind these curtains."

The balcony was thirty feet above a cement yard. Its railings had spikes, and Christy, inspired, tore down the heavy curtains.

"Come on, Doc. Tear them into strips."

They were made of tough material, and they had to tear them by holding a corner down beneath a boot and tugging with all their strength. Three fascinated prostitutes watched as they demolished the curtains. Then they knotted the strips together, and Christy, carrying the heavy escape line to the balcony, secured it by one end to a spike, and, having made sure the yard below was free of provosts, let it drop. It hung about ten feet from the cement.

"Good!" he exclaimed—then remembered his manners. He addressed the women.

"Ladies, can we help you down, or are you staying to watch the fun?"

"We go with you!"

"I'll go down first and lift 'em to the ground," Doc said at once.

"I thought you might," murmured Christy.

Doc went over the balcony and swiftly slid down the curtains. He dropped lightly to the ground, and held up his arms for the first woman to descend.

He enjoyed the operation, managing always to get his hands into the most outrageously intimate spots as he handed the women to the ground. Christy, on the balcony above, heard their diverted sniggers as he waited his turn to descend. When he finally reached the ground, there were two of the women only, and no Doc.

"Oh, no!" he lamented. "Where's my friend?"

"He go with other girl," one of the women said, grabbing his arm. "You come with me, yes? Me very obliging and certified by doctor."

The other girl now put in her bid. "Me better. Me give . . . Me . . . Me . . ." She babbled a list of delights and perversions.

Christy shook himself impatiently free and went over the iron railings of the yard. The last he saw of the women, they were pushing each other and arguing fiercely. It looked like the beginning of another fight.

The street outside was deserted. He gave up. Doc was doubtless fleeing with the woman in a *gharry* by this time. Where? There was a chance he might take her back to the hotel. In any case, it looked as though Doc was inoperative for the rest of that night. Christy stood pondering where to go. He soon knew. Keeping clear of the entrance to the Bardia, round which a large, excitable throng had collected, he found a *gharry*.

. . . . .

Sophie was alone at the bar.

"Where's Kozeta?" he asked.

She shrugged. "We have not see her today. Perhaps she is sick."

"Perhaps her ear is sore," he said, and did not bother to explain. "Goodnight. I'm tired."

Doc was not in his room.

24

Doc appeared, wet and towel-clad, in Christy's room the next morning. Christy knew him too well to expect apology, regret, or plea.

"Well," Doc asked, "how did you go?"

"Home," grunted Christy.

"I took that sheila to the Universe, you know, one of the joints on our list—and conscientiously shot my mouth off," he told Christy casually—and grinned.

"Perhaps that's a good method of working from now on," Christy replied huffily. "Split the list between us. Unilateral action. Then I don't have to worry about you and your bloody capers."

"Keep your shirt on," drawled Doc. "Anyway, Diddly-Dum said we were to stick together."

Christy leapt from the bed and pushed him, half in play, half in exasperation, across the room:

"That's why you gave me the slip last night."

"It was that sheila," Doc explained, staggering upright. "Didn't you notice what a slashing little piece she was?"

"No, I didn't! If you recall, I had very little opportunity to study them."

"Cheer up, Corpus me boy! Get some clothes on and I'll shout you some breakfast."

He left to go to his own room and dress.

I'm a liar, Christy told himself; I didn't come straight back here; I went to the Halcyon and asked the whereabouts of a sad, silent Greek girl. I'm not angry with Doc for giving me the slip: I'm angry at myself; first for telling the lie; then because I told the lie from fear of admitting to Doc that I had sought the girl, and risking his inevitable mockery. Lastly, I'm angry at myself for going back to that place, when my job there was done. It was a weakness, a softness, a sentimental, charitable tampering with a situation that should be beyond my concern, and is most certainly beyond my help. Having added that he was also a hypocrite, Christy felt better; went to the bathroom and stood for five minutes beneath the cold shower; shaved and dressed. He had almost finished when Doc, clean and immaculate, rejoined him.

. . . . .

"I don't know what plans you've got in your low mind," said Christy after breakfast, "but I am spending the day on the river. I know a good spot where we can swim and sun-bake and admire the scenery."

He turned adamantly to Doc. Doc grinned, showing his even

white teeth, and Christy noticed not for the first time, how dark the thin lips were.

"O.K.," said Doc amiably. "Let's get going. Hey, George!"

"Do you know where to go?" he asked when they were in the *gharry*. Christy gave the driver directions.

"How do you know about this place?" Doc asked.

"I learnt about it when I was here before."

"What river is it?" inquired Doc disinterestedly.

"Have a guess."

"The Zambesi?"

"Not even you could be *that* ignorant."

"Course I'm ignorant," Doc admitted amiably. "I haven't got any general knowledge, but I know all the lurks, and I know how to knock out a bit of fun, which is twice as important as knowing which river which city is on, or all the other bullshit you fill your skull with."

"How right you might be!"

"Course I'm right. Remember what I told you: eat, drink, and be merry——"

"I know, tomorrow we die. What if we don't die?"

"Then we eat, drink, and be merry again. Look at me, I don't worry about being ignorant, or having no trade . . . Well, sometimes I ask myself what I'm going to do after the war. Well, I'll swing me war record for all it's worth and work meself into something sweet and soft."

"Don't give it another thought," Christy told him. "There'll be plenty of work for people like you after the war."

"Work?" said Doc suspiciously. "What sort of work?"

"This is a bigger war than the first war, so I suppose there'll be a bigger aftermath, bigger repercussions. After the first there were revolutions or near revolutions all over Europe. Communism swallowed Russia, Fascism swallowed the rest. Who's going to swallow whom this time? How many dirty little demagogues and dictators are going to crawl out of the sewers this time?"

"What are you raving about? What's Europe or any other place got to do with me?"

"I'm speaking of you not as a person but as a type. Your kind are necessary to enforce their policies." With a wry self-mockery he added: "Just as my kind are necessary to find a sound idealistic basis for anything they do. Or rather the kind I once was."

"I'm going straight back home after the war, mate, and there won't be no revolutions there."

"No—but you'll find your opportunities. Don't worry. If I were you I'd get myself made an official of the Returned Soldiers' League, and flap the flag for all I was worth. Or charity. Now there's a good lurk! Think of all the sick, mad, or mutilated soldiers for whom you could collect money."

"You know," mused Doc, "sometimes in a mad sort of a way you talk sense."

After a while Christy dismissed the *gharry*. They alighted at the end of a street of large villas, bulking behind high walls and half hidden by palms and heavily leafed trees. A sandy lane ran away to a collection of low mud huts, where fowls wandered and children scrabbled. As they passed between the huts the children hung to their sides, holding out filthy palms, moaning and assuming pitiful expressions as they cried for *baksheesh*.

"*Shufti zubrik*," Doc challenged a small boy, and held out a coin.

The boy promptly raised his robe to display the tiny organ, and Doc delightedly handed over the coin. Christy threw a handful of coins and bid them all *salaam aleikum*.

"*Aleikum es salaam*," came the response, and they finally darted off among the hot grey labyrinth. The two men skirted the edges of a small river-made lake, left behind from an overflow, beneath a plantation of tall trees from whose higher branches large repulsive buzzards gazed down at them.

Two hundred yards ahead of them, a *dhow* seemed to be sailing across the level sea of sand, its towering, blade-like sail curved to a gentle wind. It went its stately course past a line of date palms like tattered umbrellas: a desert ship, a solid phantom. Then Doc and Christy reached the top of a sandhill and there was the river before them, an immense, shining artery of lime green.

They stood watching it. Even Doc was silenced. Small boats lay careened on the gleaming beaches. Camels watered placidly in pools. Date palms seemed almost to smoulder in the sun, but their assembled shadow was like a purple well. In the shadow squatted the still forms of men like figures in a painting. *Dhows* came past flying slim wings of white water at their low bows, wind gathered smoothly to their sails, and as each craft crossed the seething silver path of sun that lay across the river it became for a few minutes all black before their eyes, a strange and elegant silhouette.

Doc eventually became restless, for Christy still gazed, and showed no sign of motion. The moment was timeless, as was the scene they looked upon. Timeless the sun and the river and the eternal forms, the boats though moving that would never pass, the shining shores ornamented for ever by the palms, and the endless river . . . All the change ever to be seen had long ago been seen and so they stood at the eternal arrival, the timeless terminus of time. And all was hushed. Silent the river and the gems of sun that flickered across it, silent the wind in the sails and the wings of water, the men at the mast or statue-like in the bows. Christy knew that this moment and this scene was one for which his memory would ever seek its return, one of those moments, quite unheralded, that stood outside of change, experience, disillusion, or any emotion.

He murmured inwardly and moved down towards the shore, followed by Doc. They stripped there in the open and threw themselves into the green coolness of the river.

In the middle of the stream they felt the current take hold of them strongly, and they drifted down a little way until they saw a placid arm where a houseboat lay moored. Here they swam diagonally to the current and waded ashore. They walked back along the shore to their clothes and lay on the wet sand, feeling the sun dry the water swiftly from their tingling bodies.

Doc stretched his hard, muscley body.

"You have a good idea occasionally. This is grouse! Not quite Surfers' Paradise, but bloody nice."

Christy did not reply. His eyes were shut, and he seemed asleep.

"Hey!" prompted Doc.

"Shut your trap and give the other end a chance," murmured Christy with his eyes still closed. Doc grunted and obeyed. He felt the warmth of the sun investing him; a blissful tiredness crept all over him.

• • • • •

Doc was the first to wake. The sun was overhead. He reached for his shorts and took out his watch to check the time. He exclaimed and prodded the softly snoring Christy.

"Hey, Corpus, wakey, wakey."

Christy's long, lean form stirred unwillingly. He opened his eyes and half closed them again under the onslaught of the high sun.

"Wake up," repeated Doc, dumping a lump of wet sand on Christy's stomach.

Christy sat up abruptly:

"*For* what? *To* what?" he asked.

"Some bloody scran. It's two o'clock and I'm hungry."

"The nearest café is about a mile back there past those big houses."

"Well, come on!"

"I told you I was staying here all day."

"Yair, and what'll you eat? Fish from the river?"

Christy stood upright, took off his trunks, and shook sand out of them, then put them back on.

"I seem to spend most of my time pandering to your animal needs. Just hold on, Grizzleguts. I've got a plan. Give me a quid note."

A puzzled Doc obeyed. Christy wrapped the money in a handkerchief and put it between his teeth. He next tied his shirt tightly around his head.

"What's wrong with you?" asked Doc. "You going Wog or something?"

"Shut up, bastard-face."

Christy waded into deep water and was afloat.

"Wait here, fog-face. I'll only be a few minutes."

He slipped out into midstream and breast-stroked gently down with the current, working gradually towards the arm of the river where the houseboat lay. Freed of the current, he coasted slowly into the side of the houseboat.

The houseboat was moored beneath an overhanging tree and the dark, still water there was chill after the sun-warmed water of the midstream.

"Anybody home?" called Christy.

There was only silence.

He reached up, got a grip on the coaming, and hoisted himself aboard. There was a door in the middle of a long line of curtained windows. He knocked. Still silence. He tried the door and found it locked. There was another similar door forrard, but that was also locked. Presently he found a hatch, and with one tug the lock came away from the rotting woodwork.

He descended a short companionway and found himself in the silent coolness of belowdecks. He tried a door and saw only a locker full of gear. The third door along the passage was the galley.

He came across the food in a cupboard lined for coolness with tin. There were several boxes of dates, a jar of olives, a bottle of Rishon wine, biscuits, cheese, oranges, and a tin of Italian fish which was no doubt loot from Libya bought on the black market. He made a selection from the food, added the wine, and wrapped them all in the shirt. He left Doc's pound note underneath a jar in the cupboard.

He came back up top and with the bundle held on the top of his head, slipped into the water and side-stroked out into the river. Because of his decreased swimming power the current carried him well downstream before he reached the shore. He waded out to a sandhill, then sat for a few minutes resting. Five minutes later he rejoined Doc, who was dozing again.

"Lunch is served," said Christy and prodded Doc with his toe. He spread his purchases out on the shirt.

Doc stared. "Jesus Christ, where did those come from?"

"The owner of that houseboat kindly sold them to us."

Doc grinned. "That was real nice of him. Did you bring back any change?"

"No," said Christy gravely, "he charged me the full quid."

Bathed in the brilliant sun and the scent of the river sharpening their hunger, they busily ate.

Doc, with a mouthful of food, remarked generously:

"You've got initiative, I'll say that much for you."

"You are too kind. Pass the dates, Guts."

• • • • •

Made torpid by the food, they dozed through most of the afternoon. From time to time Christy opened his eyes and raised his head, as if to reassure himself—because of the silence—that the living picture was still there.

Then he opened his eyes to find that the sun had left the river. He felt chill. Beside him Doc stirred and sat up shivering. They yawned and stretched and commenced to dress. By the time they were clothed the sun was setting.

The river was a sheet of interlocking pools of red, blue, and gold. The desert that stretched between the river and sunset glowed pale rose in the evening light. Beyond, a lemon sky was streaked with saffron, orange, and gold, a sky that throbbed gently with the molten quality of its colours. The sun like a red-hot coin was already half submerged in the rose sea of the desert where shadows lay mauvely. Stark black against the sunset, the date palms seemed to have grown in stature. Camels and men stood motionless; black and huge. For yet another timeless moment, all the picture was held there. The spell, thought Christy, is that the reality is more beautiful than the legends or the visions.

The top arc of the sun pulsated once and was gone. The desert was all mauve now, the trees had retired into a mist, the river grew dark and cold. The shapes of camels and men were moving slowly, anonymously, mysteriously away. The picture was disintegrating, retiring into darkness. Strangely forlorn, a cry came to them over the water.

In silent agreement the two men put on their slouch hats and began slowly to make their way back across the sandhills, through the village, past the villas where lights shone like stars through the trees.

25

BACK in Cairo they felt tired, yet their tiredness was not the kind that demanded sleep, but rather a stimulation to break the entrancement of sun, air, and water. They showered at the hotel and rested, sitting in Christy's room clad only in towels and talking idly. Outside the evening glimmered and hummed.

Doc stretched and threw his arms wide pleasurably:

"I'd like to do something extra special tonight. Something to make this bloody city remember us by. What do you reckon, Corpus?"

"Just for once, I'm inclined to agree with you. Today we've seen the earth at its best. Now let's go and see human beings at their worst."

Doc looked suspicious at once:

"What have you got in that queer mind of yours?"

"The *burqa*."

"Now you're talking! You're not a digger till you've done the *burqa*." Suspicion took hold of him once more. "Why do *you* want to go into the *burqa*? You're always trying to keep me out of places like that."

"I feel contrary, which is because I also feel slightly unreal. I want to blot out the image of all that tranquillity and beauty with a slab of raw, brutal reality. So let's to the infamous *burqa*!"

Doc grunted vexedly.

"I don't know! Even when you do something sensible you do it for the maddest reasons."

"I can observe," went on Christy. "You can wallow. In any case, the *burqa*'s out of bounds, and if we're arrested we'll soon be released for reasons I needn't go into. Besides, I'll wager half the agents in Cairo hide out in the *burqa*."

Doc rose, and sweeping the towel from his waist, cracked it like a whip.

"That's right! We'll combine business with pleasure."

"Thus," said Christy gravely, "providing a sordid escapade with a sound moral basis."

• • • • •

Sinuous alleys of sloping shadows and anonymous doorways led into that region known as the *burqa*, a name that figured largely in the underground history of the Australian soldier: a history never to find an official historian. Across each alley, a few feet above the heads of the crowd, an enormous notice proclaimed in half a dozen languages:

OUT OF BOUNDS TO ALL RANKS BEYOND THIS POINT.

Blithely Christy and Doc walked underneath it.

Women stood and beckoned them with strange, sinful gestures; women on whose death-white faces the eyes, heavily marked with *kohl*, seemed to have been painted. Christy imagined them as creatures born without souls and therefore lacking the soul's windows. Nightly, the eyes were painted on the dead faces and forth they came to beckon, to posture, to offer their commodious flesh.

Christy observed Doc's progress. He leered back at each inveigling mask, passing revolting comments on the owner. A woman sat in a window, and as they came alongside her drew forth a round yellow breast that she held out as though offering fruit. Doc reached in and squeezed it. She grasped his arm persuasively.

"Come," she said. She pointed at the open door.

Doc reached in and drew forth her other breast, and, holding both in his palms, regarded them judiciously. Then he let them fall heavily.

"No," he told her. "I prefer 'em little and hard."

She cursed him in Arabic as they walked on.

There were few windows in these alleys that contained glass. The downstairs ones were open to the night air, allowing the women to solicit as they sat; the upper windows were latticed. Behind the window in the bare room the bed, lumpy and soiled. When a customer was persuaded in, a wooden shutter was lowered on the aperture, or a curtain drawn across; and when some minutes later he left the shutter came up again, the curtain was drawn aside, and the woman reseated herself and assumed once more the grimace that spoke in its ghastly way of the cushioning belly, the opened thighs, the pressing arms, and the co-operating motions. No joy was promised by those faces, shining in the dim light, but animal contact, swift, unprefaced penetration, spasm, and relief. Idly Christy wondered whether Doc ever felt the need for anything more than just these with his women. Not, probably, since the delusive Thelma Hopkins. Remembering all his own women, Christy realised that with the most casual of them even, there had been at least one thing about each he had liked. Kozeta, for instance. He had liked her straight shoulders, the mute and inwardly burning grief, the futile pride. He had liked her bigness of body. Somewhere at the back of his mind an idea began to glow. He gave it recognition, then returned his attention to the antics of Doc.

The alleys of the whorehouses gave way to broader, brighter, more populous streets, where music came tinkling and wailing and fat men in tarbooshes sat talking, waving, and drinking coffee from glasses. A boy like a monkey with great cow eyes ran up, saying rapidly: "You follow me for nice girls!" sped ahead a few yards, then turned to see if they were following. When he saw they were not, he came scampering back, urging them in a voice strangely guttural for his age. His dirty robe was mended, then mended again, so that it was little more than a heap of stitches.

When Doc kicked his tail he left them without resentment. That child of no innocence had few illusions about the world and men.

Christy was hoping that the day on the river had tired Doc sufficiently to keep him within bounds; but Doc strode ahead with nose out-thrust, eyes gleaming amusedly, pausing to talk with prostitutes or to consult various furtive men and boys. Doc pushed them aside. His words back at the hotel had not been uttered idly: he truly meant to give Cairo that night something by which to remember him. At last a big-eyed Armenian told him something that held his attention. Doc grabbed a handful of the man's coat: "Is this on the level, George?"

"Yes, Aussie, fair dinkum, you bet, by Jesus Christ! I know place and will take you, Aussie. Donkey and woman. Together."

Christy's heart sank. Well, he had asked for it, making that silly remark about humans at their worst. When were human beings at their worst, anyway?

"I never really believed it, this donkey and woman business," Doc told him thoughtfully. "I've heard plenty of jokers talk about it, but never met anyone who's actually seen it. What do you reckon? D'you think buggerlugs here really knows a place where it's done?"

"Probably."

"It's a new 'un on me," said Doc.

"The idea is ancient," said Christy. "A man called Lucius Apuleius wrote very amusingly about it."

"Yair? Sounds like something I ought to read. But here's the real thing, if suck-knuckle here's fair dinkum. Right-o. George, lead on, and if you're putting one over on me I'll have your balls for breakfast."

Then came trouble.

The Armenian evaporated. The reason confronted them: a patrol of provosts—Sikhs, huge, bearded, and full of business. They were led by a sergeant, who halted them and faced Christy and Doc. In English he said sternly:

"You are out of bounds. You are under arrest."

"Ay?" said Doc incredulously.

The sergeant repeated it.

Doc's face darkened with rage and violated pride. A bloody Wog trying to arrest him! Christy intervened:

"You attend to your own army. We have a reason for being here."

The sergeant's teeth flashed whitely and cynically at this. He knew their reason right enough, said the smile.

"Ready?" said Doc from the side of his mouth.

Christy gave a slight nod.

Doc swung and his fist disappeared in the Sikh's beard. The Sikh staggered and went down. Doc and Christy were already yards away, running fast.

They dived down the first alley. Behind they could hear the clatter of the provosts' boots on the stones. They sped along a narrow passage between two walls, into a courtyard, where men sat at tables and rose in alarm as they came buffeting through; out into another alley, where the crowds parted before them as the Red Sea to the children of Israel. But still behind them they could hear the sound of pursuing boots. At least the provosts were not in sight.

Looking back round the next corner, Christy saw the first of the Sikhs appear.

"They're coming round the turn!" he called and took to his heels again.

They went over a wall, scandalising a yard full of hens and sending a fat old lady who sat fanning herself on a wicker chair into hysterics; up a tree and down over the neighbouring wall, right on top of a donkey, which reared and kicked in fright as its owner gave voice to bitter resentment.

A portly Egyptian wobbling peacefully along on a bike suddenly found himself beneath his bike in the dust and rose calling Allah as a witness to the outrage and insult which had been offered him. Women in black robes turned to the wall and feared for their honour, giving thanks to God when the two madmen passed them by. A brass-pedlar cried in panic above the clashing of his wares, and a waterseller called shrill encouragement and sprayed water from his goatskin at them as they went past.

From a doorway a woman's voice said: "Aussie. Come!" And Doc, who was in the lead, did not hesitate. He plunged into the dark opening and a plump female arm pointed up some stone stairs. Christy came close behind.

At the head of the stairs stood a girl in her teens. She, too, beckoned. They found themselves in a bedroom. The girl pointed under the bed. They obeyed, and a second later a cover came down to blot out the vision of the girl's feet. They lay panting in the darkness.

Outside the door they could hear the women talking. Shouts came up dimly from the street.

"Here's a bit of luck," whispered Doc. "Rescued in the nick of time—and by a couple of sorts! I'll have one of 'em on this bed after."

"Look!" whispered Christy fiercely. "Not every woman in the *burqa*'s a crow. They've done us a big favour, so step carefully, for Christ's sake. If we're caught here they could get into trouble."

Through the walls there came to their ears the thunder of many boots.

"They're next door," said Christy.

"If they catch us, they'll bash Christ out of us," Doc told him. "They're cruel bastards, them Sikhs."

"I'll bet that sergeant's vowing some horrible revenge——"

The cover rose at the edges for a second, there was a rustling sound, a giggle, and a highly scented presence had joined them on the floor beneath the bed. It was the girl.

"Aussie!" she whispered.

Doc reached out in the darkness and found a thigh, which he squeezed.

"You're a little trimmer," he told her. "You *quayis ketir bint*."

"Control yourself," whispered Christy. "You can't do anything here—the bed's too close to the floor."

"What's the Wog for 'Thanks very much'?" Doc wanted to know.

Christy told him, and Doc repeated it to the girl, who giggled again, and said:

"Australians *quayis kitir*. You stay. Yes."

"What do you think of that?" asked Doc.

"I don't know how you do it."

"It's the lure, mate, the lure."

He heard Doc fumbling in the darkness. The giggles became squeals.

Suddenly Christy began to laugh quietly to himself. It was he who had on a whim suggested an excursion into the *burqa*; now, here they were, hiding under a bed in a strange house, taking sanctuary with two strange women, one of whom lay on the floor being manhandled by Doc, who couldn't mount her because the bed was far too near the floor.

Oh, God! he thought, the tears running down his face, there are compensations for being saddled with Doc Home.

"What's wrong with you?" Doc was asking him.

"I'm lonely," gasped Christy. "I want someone under here with me too."

As if in answer, the edges of the bed-cover rose again, and the owner of the plump arm began to push herself, grunting, underneath the bed.

"Oh, Gawd!" gurgled Doc. "Don't tell me prayers are never answered. This must be our lucky night."

Christy gave a large bottom a friendly pat. He found that the plump woman was trying to whisper something to him:

"Proovoo—they gone."

He listened. The sounds of boots the other side of the wall had ceased.

"She's just given the all-clear," he told Doc, speaking in his normal voice.

"Good!" said Doc briskly. "Come on, Queen Farida."

They crawled out thankfully from underneath the bed.

The room was large, and looked old and solid, the floor of stone, the walls patterned with coloured tiles. The bed was enormous. Of ornate, black-painted iron, it had a huge brass knob at the top of each post, and a row of smaller ones, like a litter, in between. The women, whom Christy took to be mother and daughter, were regarding them with favourable expressions.

The woman, of about forty-five but handsomely plump and by no means past her prime, wore a plain black dress. Her features were Syrian. The daughter was very much to Doc's taste; slim, long-legged, small-breasted, with black hair that had the sheen of a crow's feathers. Her violent blue dress was obviously something of the mother's made over, and on top of it she wore, of all things on a hot night in Cairo, a scraggy fur bolero.

Without speaking, the pair of them stood looking at Christy and Doc as though they were two favoured male relations.

"Australians very good," spoke the mother at last.

"You are Syrian?" asked Christy.

"Lebanon." She nodded.

"You are very good too," he told her, "hiding us from the Indian provosts. Do you understand what I am saying?"

She nodded again, with an earnest frown.

"I understand," she told him. "I learn English."

Is this a whorehouse of two?—thought Christy. Mum looked experienced, the daughter was not exactly innocent. If they were going to whore again tonight——

"Look," he mumbled to Doc, so the women could not hear, "if we're going to cavort with these two, it better be quick, and not for the night, which seems to be their idea. We've got a few calls to make."

The girl broke in, speaking rapidly:

"You stay. Wait. We show you . . ."

She looked for help to her mother. There had been nothing coquettish in her invitation to stay. Both of them seemed not only at a loss for words, but at a loss as to how many of the known English words they ought to speak. Christy by this time distinctly smelt a rat—of a colour undetermined.

All of a sudden the woman's eyes brightened; she spoke to the daughter in excited Arabic, and the girl ran with a glad laugh from the room. The woman smiled at them reassuringly and complacently.

Presently the girl returned, her fur coat looking rather like the feathers of an outraged hen, carrying a bundle of clothes which she displayed to the two men. The bundle consisted of a digger's hat, an Australian Army tunic, and a webbing belt. Holding the bundle up to them significantly, she indicated the house at large, and her mother said:

"Aussie here. You stay. Please."

"Well," marvelled Doc, "what do you know? Some bastard's cut himself off a very tasty slice of cake. Wait!" he told the woman. "You couldn't get me out of here now with a team of wild horses. Well, what do you know!"

Christy nodded several times vigorously, at which the woman, with a gracious gesture, beckoned them from the room and into another.

Here there were a bead curtain, tiles even more lurid, a huge pot-plant, and on the walls those highly-coloured, apocalyptic sacred pictures which abound in the Lebanon. There was a table spread with a cloth of silk in some Persian design, several pieces of brass, and on a small oil-stove the inevitable blackened pot of coffee. She motioned them to be seated, and with a hearty, gladdened air both mother and daughter proceeded to put food and drink in front of them: bread like pancakes, olives, dates, rice, and cardamom seeds. The mother gave them coffee in cups without handles, and disappeared for some minutes into an alcove that reeked of cooking, emerging with several skewers of *kebab*, which she placed proudly before them. With a brilliant, comprehending smile she produced finally a bottle of *arak* and poured them each a measure in small glasses.

The two men remembered that they had not eaten since two o'clock that day. With grateful, princely gestures at the women, they commenced to drink and eat. Mother and daughter stood by and watched them with a complacent, conspiratorial air. Christy still smelt a rat, but not a foetid rat.

There was apparently an Australian staying in the place. Why just one? Perhaps the mother worked the daughter as a prostitute, receiving male customers into the house only where she could keep an eye on things. Not many Australians were on leave in Cairo these days, with things so sticky at El Alamein; the temporary boarder was probably a base-walloper—or a deserter. That was it! It explained the curious behaviour of the two women: the eagerness to have them stay and yet not say too much.

"You know something," he told Doc, "I think there's a bloke staying here who's adrift."

"Which one of them's he sleeping with?" Doc asked instantly.

"Ask them," grunted Christy.

There was silence for some minutes while they chewed. Doc found the *kebab* very much to his taste, and asked Christy what it was. Christy told him round a mouthful of it. Finally, replete, they both leant back and sighed.

"You know," said Doc expansively, "this Wog food ain't too bad—not too bad at all. I enjoyed that."

He looked up and ran his eyes shamelessly over the two women. He settled them on the daughter, and winked. Her face was sallow, over-inhabited by the nose, but her eyes in their dark beauty made one blind to the mannish size of it. The teeth which smiled back at Doc were white and pointed. Wiry, vixenish, fiery, she was bound to attract Doc. It seemed to Christy that Doc's addiction to frail bodies was akin to the fascination that birds had for cats. He wanted something he could break, something to capture and contain. Yes, there was sadism in Doc, in the sheen of his narrow dark eyes, the rapacious curve of his nose, the savagery of his white smile.

The women had seated themselves now on a sofa draped with a bright red cloth, side by side. The mother essayed further conversation:

"Proovoo *musha quayis*. No catch. Good!"

She gave a warm, low giggle.

Doc, picking his teeth, pointed at the girl and said:

"*Quayis bint*. How much?"

He's off! thought Christy. But the girl merely put her hand over her mouth and giggled louder than ever, while the mother agreed the daughter was indeed a fine girl, and liked the big sergeant very much.

"Looks," observed Christy dryly, "as though you're going to get it for love."

"The lure, mate, the lure!"

"They're waiting for something," said Christy sharply. "It's not just our bright eyes. It could be the Aussie's coming, and it could be something else."

Doc's eyes became dark gashes. He looked at the women without smiling.

"Do you reckon they've shelved us? Is the provosts what they're waiting for?"

"Use your head. They haven't been out of our sight since they hid us. The girl was under the bed and Mum was just outside the door until she joined the party. No, they wouldn't get anything out of turning us in."

"Do you reckon they've got a mob coming to do us over for our dough?" Doc took off his webbing belt. "They'll get a bit of a reception if that's the caper." He fingered the buckle, which could lay a man's head open.

"Wait and see. But I think it's this Australian. I'll put money on there being a bloke adrift living here."

Christy studied the women. There was no guilt in their faces. Only a gratification at their presence. Suddenly the mother lifted her finger and assumed a listening pose. She spoke in Arabic to the daughter. Both looked expectant. The mother half rose, but Christy motioned her gently to stay where she was, and, rising himself, went and opened the door. The stairs were lit only dimly. There was footsteps below. Someone was whistling, and as Christy recognised the tune, he felt a wave of relief and amusement. For the tune was "The Road to Gundagai". In the muddy pool of light below a figure clad in a grubby white suit and with a *tarboosh* on its head began to mount the stairs, still whistling "The Road to Gundagai". Quietly, Christy stepped back inside and closed the door.

"I was right," he told Doc. To the two women he said:

"Your Australian's coming."

They broke into broad smiles. The whistling was loud and shrill now. It ceased abruptly. The boots halted outside the door. It swung open. The figure in the white suit and the *tarboosh* stood revealed. For a few seconds Christy and Doc sat with wide eyes and open mouths, stupefied. Then, together, they roared:

"*Horrible John!*"

26

IT couldn't be Horrible John sitting there talking expansively to them, with all the aplomb of the head of a household; grubby suit, red *tarboosh*, a purveyor of dubious goods, a procurer of pleasures, such as teem in Cairo, to the very life. It was a fantasy! They had had too much sun that day. There had been something in the *arak*.

But Horrible John sat back on the sofa, his women flanking him adoringly, and told them:

"Yers didn't think I meant it when I said I was gonna shoot through. Well, here I am. Look at the tasty old result!"

"But the bloody provosts caught you!" cried Doc appealingly.

"Well," replied Horrible John serenely, "as yers can see, I got away."

"Horrible," announced Christy, "revolt me though you do, I must say I feel glad to see you at large—and"—Christy's eyes indicated the women—"so well set up."

Horrible John inclined his head in a superior manner. Doc hid his face in his hands.

"Too much has been happening," he muttered. "First this mad bloody leave—now running into Horrible like this." He raised his face and, grinning ferociously, went on: "Horrible, you've got my vote. You're the greatest lurk-artist this side, or any bloody side of the black stump. Now drop the bullshit and tell us how you did it. Tell us how in the name of Christ you ended up in this place, with a couple of sheilas eating out your hand."

"Very well," acceded Horrible John Jones with the same lordly air, and Christy hastily swallowed a shout of mirth. Then he began to talk boastfully, rapidly, like the Horrible John they knew:

"Yers know Doggy Drummond in C Company, don't yers? . . ."

They did. An incredibly ugly man who had been in all sorts of trouble with Horrible John. The Colonel had seen to it that they stayed in separate companies.

". . . Well, as you know, Doggy and me have been in the field detention camp before, and we worked out a way of getting out some time ago, ready for the next time one of us got lumbered. Yer see, Diddly-Dum had told us that the next time it'd be Jerusalem, but you're held in a local detention camp until your court-martial, or until they're ready to haul you off to Jerusalem. So it meant working fast, as soon as they stuck you behind wire—'cos no bastard ever got out of Jerusalem.

"Well, after I gets remanded, Doggy hangs around Battalion Headquarters and gets it out of Bastable where I've been taken. It was only five miles down the coast road, a couple of big Indian tents with a lot of dannaert wire round 'em and a provost on guard at the gate. While you're in one of them joints, just on remand or doing a short stretch, they'll let visitors come and see you.

"This is the way we worked it. The provosts on guard are changed every two hours. So Doggy hops a truck and about three minutes to four that afternoon, just before the guard's due to be relieved, Doggy arrives at the gate and says to the provost: 'I've come to see Private Horrible Jones. He's a sitter for a long stretch and I've got some letters from his dear old Mum he always carried with him.' 'In you go,' says the copper. 'Here,' says Doggy, 'if you're relieved before I'm out don't forget to tell your mate I'm visiting.' 'I won't,' says the provost. In comes Doggy. We waits till we see the provost relieved, then I puts on Doggy's hat and goes out to the new guard at the gate. 'I'm the joker who's been visiting Private Jones,' I says. 'O.K.,' he says without even looking at me. 'Off you go.' And that was one order I obeyed. There's a truck passing and I thumb it and hop aboard—and I stand up in the back and yell: 'You silly bastard, I'm Horrible John Jones!' . . . And that, gents, is how Uncle Horrible escaped from the mug coppers."

And Horrible John sat back, lit a cheroot that reeked like a compost heap, and surveyed them with a benign and grandiose air.

"The coot's a genius," breathed Doc.

"The genius is also a coot," said Christy. "He left Doggy holding the can."

"I foggin' well didn't!" cried Horrible John righteously. "Doggy had a yarn all ready about going out to the pissaphone and finding me gone when he came back. Yers didn't hear anything about him, did yers?"

"No, we must have come on leave soon after all this."

"Leave!" repeated Horrible John. "Yers are ack-willy, aren't yers? Nobody's gettin any leave."

They showed him their leave passes, but cut his congratulations short. There was a lot more they needed to be told.

"That was a bit silly, yelling out at the provost like that," said Doc.

"Not on your life," said Horrible John. "Yer see, Doggy had ripped out the ignition leads behind the dashboard of their truck before he came in, when no one was looking. Besides, I leant over and had a peep into the cabin of the truck I'd hailed. They were only two privates, so I told 'em what I'd just done, and they laughed themselves sick and went like the hammers of hell, all the way to Alex."

"Now," went on Doc, settling himself with the air of a man getting down to the vital business, "tell us how you finished up here."

His wave indicated the room and the two women.

Horrible John's fat, self-congratulating grin was becoming unbearable.

"Mum and me are old friends. Aren't we, love?" He grinned

sideways uxoriously, the woman grasped his arm simperingly and smiled; and Christy could not decide whether it was pathetic or farcical.

"Yer see," proceeded Horrible John, "me and Doggy found this place last time we was on leave here. You remember we won a packet at the swy? Well, the first night we're here young Sophita here"—he indicated the girl—"accosts us in the street. When she tells us that there's someone else at home we go with her. I sleep with Mum here—her name's Jamfieph—and Doggy with young Flossie, but the next day Doggy wanders off to get blotto and find another sheila. Me, I stay with Mum. I stayed here for the rest of me leave and the week's ack-willy I had. I'd got plenty of oscar and I looked after her. She was able to go out and buy good tucker and grog, and young Flossie comes in off the streets. They're Lebanese, yer see, Jammy's husband got killed in an air-raid and she used to send Flossie out to earn the rent occasionally . . . Do you remember I got into a blue for losing me pay-book? Well, I didn't, I sold it to a bloke for a hundred quid, a Kiwi who'd been over here before the war and knew the lingo, and deserted. He was doing all right for himself one way and another, living on some rich Wog woman at Gizeh.

"Mum's been looking after that dough for me."

"You mean to say you trusted her?"

"Yair, of course I did. I'd left her a few quid to get by on and I told her I'd be back. I also told her if she touched that dough I'd cut her throat. But she's pretty fair dinkum—aren't yer, love?"

Again the exchange of conjugal smirks.

"There's a dirty big bed in the next room," said Horrible John grandiloquently.

"We know, she hid us underneath it."

"Well, that's ours."

"Does Sophita share it with you?" asked Christy. "It's big enough."

"She's got a cubby-hole behind a curtain. She used to sleep with Mum before I came. She can't grumble, she don't have to go out on the street now, anyhow."

"How about me and her?" Doc asked with a sly, suggestive grin.

Horrible John held his cheeroot out elegantly and pursed his lips masterfully:

"You'll be sweet, sport. Flossie don't sleep with just anyone these days. This," he declared with a grotesque air of virtue, "is a respectable household."

The only way to bring this scene into the confines of reality, thought Christy, is to scream with laughter. He refrained. There was more to come.

"How're you making out now?" asked Doc.

"Well, I gave Mum some money and she got the tools to make

cakes and sweets. Like most Lebanese women, she's a bloody fine cook. I do a little trading here and there"—he winked—"and I pretend to be a Gypo and show some pommy soldier around—take him to a low joint, you know the sort of stuff. I get along. She and Flossie take the cakes and things out and sell them. A Greek with a stall along here, joker called Sam, he lets 'em put up a table."

There was a short silence. Doc was grinning, Christy was shaking violently.

"And now," said Horrible John, "I want to know how yers come to be here, and how yers come to be hiding underneath my bed."

"We got chased by provosts," Doc explained. "Sikhs. They stopped us and tried to arrest us. I king-hit the sergeant and we up and off. As we came past here with these Sikhs on our hammer Mum here called us in and hid us under the bed."

"Now ain't that just like Mum!" exclaimed Horrible John, beaming tenderly at her. "Loves Aussies! Yer see, her husband was a black-marketeer and used to buy most of his stuff from diggers. Then I came. No, she won't hear a word against the Anzacs."

"Look!" said Christy abruptly, "you not doing anything silly, are you? Your secret's safe with us but you're not doing anything, well, wrong?"

"How do yer mean?"

"He means anything against the war effort, you know, no subversive stuff or anything," Doc explained.

Horrible John was scandalised:

"Most certainly not! I'm no bloody traitor! Just because I've deserted that don't mean I'd do anything against the poor old King. Have a heart!"

"Well, that's all right then," conceded Doc. He looked around him again, the envy plain on his face. Doc would like something like this, thought Christy; for a time at least. But Doc would never desert, never even go A.W.L. For Doc had his pride; Doc had not been tolerated, buffeted, and despised by society sufficiently to have no pride left in regard to it. His stripes meant something to him. Being a member of a famous fighting division had meant to Horrible John—precisely Nil.

In his way, he supposed, Horrible John had found himself. Which was more than could be said for Arnold Christy.

27

THERE came the celebration. Horrible John sent Flossie out for drink and Jamfieph brought cakes and sweets from her store. Doc took the girl on his knee, Horrible John and he toasted each other, and Christy sat silently by, rather less amused now, but still intrigued by the preposterous situation.

After half an hour, and several *araks*, Horrible John told Doc:

"We'll have to arrange a sort for Corpus. That's only fair."

Christy laughed loudly at this.

"Thanks, Horrible, but Doc and I had an appointment. At least one of us had better keep it."

"Oh, yes," said Doc with a calculating look. "You don't mind, do you?" he asked Christy.

Christy rose, grinning.

"Not really. If you're set on tom-catting again tonight, here is as safe as anywhere. Well, Horrible, I think I'd better drift."

He said good night to Jamfieph and Sophita, and Horrible John showed him hospitably to the door.

"Now don't forget where I live," were his parting words.

Laughing silently, Christy assured him he wouldn't.

Come again and be my guest, the guest of Horrible John Jones, under-privileged bastard from a home who had joined the army as the only way ever to afford to travel; fought till he considered his price to be paid and then deserted. Horrible John, now gone Wog, imitation-Wog, picker up of sharp money, doted on by a plump matron from Tartus old enough to be his mother.

And why not? Jamfieph and Horrible John had perhaps come together by instinct: Two people both so ill-used as to have no use for pride: he to desert his country's cause, she to send her daughter on to the streets. They both knew the meaning of a necessity that overruled all else. She was probably the first person in his entire life he had had reason to trust; and she had proved—herself to him, holding his bankroll till he returned, trusting him to return.

Christy began to think of Eva. Doc would have yearned after her. Tall, legs and thighs so straight and smooth, long, swaying waist, small breasts, and dark hair like a tempest. She had trusted him to return, and he had returned, only to leave again. He was sure he would marry her eventually; he thought of no other, hungered for no other. But in your youth you think you can find the Answer somewhere out there in the maze of your journeyings; somewhere among the trees rushing by, in the colossal greenery of the mountains that enclosed the rails. All the immensity and the loveliness, the grandeur of peak and the unguessed world of sky beyond *had* to be meaningful. In the vast, tortured, heroic territories of Beethoven the Answer was being cried for.

And in the end he had come back to find that Eva had wearied and gone; married to a German called Blomberg and gone back with him to his vineyard in the Barossa Valley. Eva had wanted fulfilment, love, the expenditure of passion; even the second-best rather than wait for the face to droop and the belly no longer able to produce; she wanted physical possessions and pregnancy and the special power that belongs only to a woman with a man.

The Persian from Khorassan had been right, nine hundred years ago. There is no answer, and all the saints and sages are mocked.

With the silence, the No-Answer, went also Eva.

Probably now she was fat and the mother of several. Her husband unfaithful. She had had it all by this time: pain, humiliation, illness, yearning, anxiety. Lines radiating from the corners of the eyes, another chin swaying below the first . . . But she was *being*.

Well, you could always *be*, in the simplest, crudest terms like Doc and Horrible John. Drink like a rectifier to freeze the thought and heat the blood; a woman like an aperient.

He stopped at the Halcyon after finding his way out of the *burqa*. Neither Sophie nor Kozeta was to be seen. He stayed for a while, drinking *ouzo* swiftly, so swiftly it hurt his throat. The place was crowded and sweat hung in the blue air like sour dew. He left, warm and unsteady.

At the hotel, Madam and the dark girl Doc had rolled in their first hour there was leaning on the desk as they talked. He waved at them grandly, pinched Madam's cheek and grasped a handful of the girl's bottom as Doc had. Madam smiled and the girl's eyes lit. He mounted the stairs, and several steps above them turned around. Madam watched him reproachfully at his sudden loss of dignity.

"Tell Ibrahim!" he shouted foolishly. "I want him to get one or two things for me."

Hc found his room mainly by instinct. Hc sat on thc bcd and watched the walls rotate warmly and pleasantly. Presently Ibrahim entered:

"I can do for you something, *effendi*?"

"Yes, by Christ you can!" He drew several notes from his shirt. "Here! Go out and come back with good strong drink, *arak*, *ouza*, peppermint . . . and a girl. Got it?"

Ibrahim took the notes greedily. "I go quick." He moved to the door, passing the girl from downstairs as he went out of the door. She stood and looked at Christy, her body leant at an angle that declared the whole curve of belly, breasts out-thrust acutely, legs crossed to draw the skirt in close to the crutch.

"Ibrahim!" he called. "*Maaleesh* the girl—just the drink."

28

WHEN Christy woke he showered, then went to Doc's room, to find it still empty. He returned to his own, where he found the dark woman arriving with his coffee and rolls. She smiled without speaking and left. He finished the coffee and rolls and went out into a bright morning. He felt in need of a walk. There were a taste in his mouth, a feeling in his head he thought a walk might get rid of.

He walked a fairly long way. He wondered where Doc was and at what time the girl had left his room. I must have been very drunk, he thought. He remembered the encounter with Horrible John and laughed again.

He found himself leaning over the bridge at Kasr El Nid. A pair of boys came up, chattering, to worry him until he chased them off. He was not the only one looking at the greeny-brown water. He looked along the rail. He found his attention held by a female ear.

He could see little else because of a fat Egyptian between them. It was an ear which had been pierced but now carried no ear-ring. He moved nearer. He recognised the shoulders and the proud set of the head. Opening the pocket of his shirt, he drew out the little gold ear-ring and approached. She did not even glance up as he came to stand beside her. He held the ear-ring out in his palm.

"You left this, Kozeta."

She turned swiftly, surprised, and as she recognised him her face lit up. She looked down at the ear-ring in his palm.

"I brought it to the Halcyon," he said, "but you weren't there."

"I have not been back."

"What are you doing? Have you got something else?"

She shrugged and looked stubbornly at the water. Her eyes held no light.

"I suppose I shall go back," she said. "There, or somewhere else."

Looking not at her but at the water, he said carefully:

"It is difficult enough without money—but with no papers . . ."

Her expression was neither bitter nor angry; it seemed to him she had lost some of her pride.

"And no friends," she added.

"And worst of all, no hope," he said.

She looked up angrily at this.

"Why do you say that?" she asked. "Are you trying to frighten me?"

"I think you have lost hope since I saw you last. You have resigned yourself to something."

"I have been thinking," she told him bitterly. "I have seen what is real. It would have been better if I had stayed in Greece."

"With the Germans? You need time to settle here. Perhaps after a time you would find something better to do than—well, the Halcyon."

"The only friend I have is Sophie. She is not the friend I need."

"Do we ever get the friends we need?"

It was not said in this ordinary tones, and she looked at him thoughtfully.

"The way the world is," he continued, "we all need so much that there is no one to give all we need. To scorn all you need can be done only by the strongest—and the strongest are the loneliest. I'm not sure I want to be as lonely as all that."

"You are not like your friend," she said softly. "You are a man of many hungers."

The words stirred, embarrassed him. Coming from one who should have been blind to all misery but her own in the ordinary way of things. Yet there was perception in her glance. Compassion. He felt as though he were robbing her of something.

They looked at each other without speaking for half a minute. He liked her proud comeliness more than ever. He wondered what she saw. He answered his own speculation, regretfully, hopelessly: a man on the verge of middle age with not much of a life expectation who had lost too many of his faiths.

Yet he wanted to declare something; if possible, do something for her.

"I'm glad I've met you," he said at last, and the words limped. "If it had not been for the war, we would not even know of each other's existence. It is best to look at it like that—an accident brought about by the war. One of many such accidents." He stopped, remembering the idea that had formed dimly in his mind not many hours ago.

"Look," he said grasping her arm. "Will you meet me later? Say, at two o'clock?"

She nodded.

"Do you know the Café de l'Est?"

"Near King Fuad Street?"

"Correct. I want you to meet me there at two. Will you?"

"Yes."

"Good!"

"But you are suddenly in a hurry. You have remembered something?"

"That's right. I've remembered something."

• • • • •

"Yes?" said the major's voice.

"Christy here."

"Yes?" The voice sharpened. "What has happened?"

"I've lost all my money. I'll need some more."

"How did you manage that?"

"I don't know for certain. I think perhaps my pocket was picked in one of these places."

"Probably. The sergeant warned you explicitly about that."

"You forget we're supposed to behave carelessly."

"I forget nothing, including that you Australians are pretty sharp."

"What do I do?" demanded Christy. "Report back to my unit?"

"You do the job you were sent here for." The major's voice was unfriendly now. "Do you know the Hotel Des Roses?"

"Yes."

"The sergeant will meet you there in half an hour with more cash. Be there."

"Yes, sir. Good-bye."

"Oh, to the devil with you," said the major.

The sergeant made him sign for the fresh money. Christy did not even thank him. He hurried away, rather amused at his lack of any feeling of shame.

. . . . .

At the Café de l'Est he found Kozeta waiting for him at one of the tables in the garden behind, beneath the vines where the sun came down through in gold wraiths. He sat down and ordered drinks. When they arrived he pressed the money into her hands holding it there while he spoke:

"Please don't argue about this, or be offended, or feel proud. I have earned this money, more than earned it—so you needn't fear about it being stolen. It is quite a large amount. If you are careful it should last you some time, long enough for you to do something better than hanging around a place like the Halcyon, and find other friends than Sophie. I ask you to take it. I shall have no use for it."

He half expected her to give him one of her proud looks. But she was gazing down at the back of Christy's hand that held the money against her palm. Suddenly she looked up, and she was smiling.

"Yes," she said very gently, "I shall take it, with my greatest thanks."

"Good!" he cried.

She patted his hand.

"This," she said, "this is one of your hungers."

"You can put it any way you like—now you've accepted the money."

"I am glad," she told him, "that the war has done this much."

He rose and told her abruptly:

"I've got to go now."

"So soon! Promise you will not go to the Halcyon again. You were very foolish with drink last time. You told me military things you should not have told me."

"Did I! I hope you didn't repeat them."

"I shall say nothing. You can trust me."

This, he thought, is the worst irony. If she only knew why I really went to the Halcyon.

"I think I can."

"When shall we meet again?" she asked.

"We shan't. There is no use in it. I'm—I'm going back. Good-bye."

She still sat there as he walked away. The sun was striking blue fire in her hair.

29

HE was still laughing at himself when he walked into the hotel and found Doc there talking to the dark woman at the desk.

"Where've you been, Corpus?"

"Round and about. Have a good time?"

"Bloody lovely. You just missed Horrible. He came back with me."

"I'm desolated," murmured Christy.

"I'll pay Horrible," said Doc admiringly. "I'll pay him round the back."

"Forget Horrible," Christy told him with a sharpness that made Doc raise his eyebrows and grin. He looked at Madam and found her smiling too. It was a confiding, conspiring smile. I'll bet she knows all about last night, thought Christy; and suddenly was sick of everything, including himself.

"I'm glad this leave is nearly over," he muttered.

"You're off your nut," Doc told him.

They went out and had something to eat, then returned to the hotel and slept through the afternoon. At night, they dressed clean and went forth again, and found their last and most productive dive—the Mareka. It was so productive they disregarded the rest of their list.

The Mareka was on the fringes of the *burqa*. It was designated by a small sign above an unpromising doorway. They descended old, winding stone stairs and found themselves not in the haze, the noise, the odours they had expected, but in a cold-smelling silence. The place resembled a crypt, all archways and pillars, with spidery tables strewn among them. It was as dark as a crypt. A long time ago it probably had been a crypt.

There the resemblance ended. The hush was neither solemn nor meditative.

"The joint's shut," said Doc.

Christy did not comment. He was trying to find the wavelength of the atmosphere, identify the melancholy call-sign. In the gloom the tables seemed to be crawling about like spiders. The place, he thought, was haunted by tired old sins. It was evil without stature, sinister without awakening fear. It was full of wasted years and things surrendered for money and hopes given up.

And the lights went on.

"Gentlemen," spoke a voice quietly, "my most earnest welcomes."

The small man who approached had great gazing gazelle eyes, large rounded nose, and very little chin. The cream linen suit he wore had plainly once belonged to a larger man. The hand that seemed to cringe at his thighs was dough-coloured, chubby as a baby's.

"What's the strong of this joint?" demanded Doc brusquely. "Not an undertaker's is it?"

"We undertake almost anything here, Sergeant," the little man replied a softly as a baby's sigh. "But you have come for pleasure, I can see." Without any motion of the slim shoulders or any change in the mournful eyes, the little hands waved and the thick red lips added: "Welcomes once again. My name is Albert and I will understand your needs. The wine? The women? The song? My real name is Ayoub Fanous and I am an ancient Egyptian."

"You're *what*?" said Doc.

"I am a descendant of the ancient people of Egypt. My ancestors were here in the days of the Pharaohs."

"Go *hon*!" chuckled Doc. "Come to look at you, you do look a bit like the Sphinx."

"I am," proceeded Albert humbly, "a Copt."

"Bad luck," said Doc consolingly. "Who copped you?" He guffawed.

"Shut up, you animal," Christy told him. "This gets interesting."

Albert suddenly moved in his skinny entirety. He reached a table and pulled out two chairs.

"Soldiers, please to be seated." He moved to a large grubby curtain in the wall and pulled it to reveal a bar stacked with a kaleidoscope of strange bottles. From under the counter he produced a gramophone, which he wound; then he lowered the arm on to a record. There was a scratch, a lurch, and a voice raucously begged someone to "do do do what you've just done done once more, baby."

"Well, I'll be fogged," said Doc. "Anyhow," he asked Christy, "what *is* a Copt?"

"A religious sect."

"Him? Eye-oob fanny-arse, or whatever he called himself? Him religious? He looks as cunning as a lavatory rat to me."

"All agog to take down naïve and unwordly people like you," remarked Christy.

"I'd like to see him."

"You may yet, you may."

Albert drifted across with two drinks that smelt strong and sweet.

"With the compliments of Ayoub Fanous," he told them.

Albert bent over them as they drank the syrupy greenish liquid.

"The Mareka," he explained, "begins late. Midnight, soldiers, you will see many things." The huge eyes rolled. "But wait! I can get for you now, by virtue of a message, two girls to make you company." He raised a deferential eyebrow and waited.

Christy shrugged. He was ceasing to believe in their job. It was all like a silly dream. He could no longer believe that armies fought except with weapons and missiles. The shadow-game of the cities and the lonely places; the stealthy getting-to-know and the letting-know (such as their own) were all a futile taradiddle danced on the fringes of the advance, the retreat, the capture and the carnage.

All he saw now was a dark head and a straight nose, an ear from which an ear-ring was torn, set like some glowing fresco against the sunshot water. He remembered consolingly his deception of the major. Well, something, perhaps useful and good, had been stolen from the farce. He felt little like drinking, less like whoring; yet he must, just to make quite certain, mustn't he, that the bloody Afrika Corps were ready and waiting in their might on the day the Fifty-Fifth swept in on them with their bayonets bared and the guns rapping at the gates of eternity?

He threw his arm wide, recklessly.

"Good boy, Albert! Go and round up a couple of tasty young sluts."

Doc stared at him. Then, "I echoes them sentiments," he told Albert.

Watching Albert walk obediently away, he confided to Christy:

"He's a queen."

"He's a bit of everything," said Christy.

Albert came back within minutes. Somewhere, behind one of the several curtains, they had heard his voice like a draught in a corridor. Christy invited him to be seated.

"You're a Copt you said."

For the first time Albert lowered his eyes. The lids came down like two smooth shells. The voice murmured:

"Alas, I am a Fallen Copt."

"You sure you weren't pushed?" asked Doc.

Albert looked up at Christy piteously.

"I have sinned," he said. "Sinned with might. My dreams are full of my sins. I have done all sins."

My God! thought Christy, the little wretch might actually have a conscience. Lucifer, he thought, would despise Ayoub Fanous.

"Soon you will meet many people in here," Albert told them. "Strange people, unhappy people. There are sometimes police . . . I think," he added slowly, "that soldiers have leave passes."

Silently they drew them forth and displayed them. Doc leant forward and said to Albert earnestly:

"Now listen here, Albert. You were right. It's wine, women, and song for us and not too much bloody singing. Now you look after us, see? We've got plenty of money, and we don't care if we spend the lot 'cos very soon we'll be in the middle of a very big batt——"

Christy took his cue here and motioned Doc into silence. At that instant, Albert's eyes shone fleetingly; then the lids dropped down on them in swift concealment.

This is it! thought Christy. Something tingled at the back of his brain. Hitherto they had been in the dark; shooting off their mouths in drunken indiscretion and trusting that sooner or later those indiscretions would find their mark. But of Albert he was as certain as he was of his own name. Doc's carefully punctuated slip of the tongue had sent something new into the glossy, prune-coloured eyes of Ayoub Fanous the Fallen Copt. He wondered whether Doc shared his certainty. It didn't much matter. Doc had suspected Albert on sight.

"Soldiers," pledged Albert with an air that was nothing less than reverent, "I will look after you like a brother." His great eyes shone before the holiness that was cash. "The girls who come," intoned Albert fervidly, "are of great beauty and affection. There are others. There are"—here he lowered his lids and his voice together and looked immeasurably discreet—"other things . . ."

"Yair?" cried Doc with an eagerness that was only part feigned.

"You will see," breathed Albert, his face shining in ecstasy like his eyes. He took up their empty glasses and drifted towards the bar as though he were approaching an altar.

Presently there came the sounds of light heels on the stairs and two girls came into the *Mareka.* Albert held out his arms to them.

"They are here," he said somewhat unnecessarily. The two girls approached.

The one in the white dress with the slits at the sides was dark-haired with a round brown face, bold dark eyes; emphasising her hips as she walked, she made as if by instinct for Christy.

The other who made for Doc had henna-ed hair that fell to her shoulders, was very nearly flat-chested, and wore long metal ear-rings. Her skin was dark and her face was sharp and urchin-like.

They both smiled as Albert spoke, halting, then both grabbing near-by chairs and seating themselves with Christy and Doc. Albert softly introduced them. The dark one was called Gloria; the redhead Albert introduced as Juliet. The men welcomed them expansively, and then there was Albert who had placed drinks before them all—and then there was no Albert.

Gloria asked Christy: "What is your name, Australian?"

"Call me Bill," he told her.

"All Australians are called Bill."

"I'm Doc," said Doc, and eyed Juliet wickedly.

And I'll bet neither of your names is Juliet or Gloria, thought Christy. Well, here goes! Advance, Don company! He shifted his chair nearer to Gloria who smiled welcomingly. Her smile was attractive and unfeigned.

Two more women came down the stairs, seated themselves at a table and without as much as a glance at the four already there, leaned over looking into each other's face, talking low and vehemently. One was gross and middle-aged and wore a plain dark frock that was cut as severely as an overall. Her face was without make-up, her hair was groomed like a man's. The woman who faced her was waspish, haggard, with girlish movements and quivering lips.

"Emile and Roberta are quarrelling again," said Gloria looking over. "They are husband and wife," she confided to Christy. "Roberta is very jealous."

Doc turned around to gaze at them interestedly.

"I'm going to enjoy myself tonight." he said.

"Oh, yes!" giggled Juliet and grasped his arm.

Doc pinched her cheek and pouted at her fondly. She giggled again, but her eyes were sharp. Christy had the feeling that Albert had already told her to be watchful.

They settled down to some steady drinking. Gradually the place filled up. Women wandered in, women with faces they had seen gesturing from those apertures in the *burqa*. A man sat near them in a waisted coat with painted lips, leered at Doc, who pretended to vomit into his beer. Grubby little men whose pockets hung down with the weight of their dubious wares. Women with the shiny, painted eyes of the drug-taker.

And every now and then they saw Albert, as he put a fresh record on, or came out from behind one curtain to disappear behind another. What had been the cold-smelling silence was now the blue, pungent spirals of Turkish tobacco and the murmurs and shouts of several tongues.

Doc was leaning back in his chair, toasting all those whose eyes met his, while Juliet leaned over, felt his biceps greedily, wiped lipstick against the lobe of his ear. To Christy, his savage white grin seemed to waver and swim and he had to close his eyes for a second to get that familiar, predatory countenance focused.

He found Gloria speaking to him, as though from a distance:

"You will be in Cairo on long leave?"

"A few more days," he told her.

She nodded calculatingly.

"You like Juliet and me?"

He fell into his part and squeezed her knee:

"You're a couple of beautsh."

She bit her lip carefully.

"You and the Doc would like to stay with Juliet and me all the time for your leave?"

"That'sh what we want—to stay with you and Juliet."

He leaned over and put his wet lips against her neck.

Suddenly she rose. "Juliet!" she said, Juliet looked up. She motioned with her head and Juliet rose too. "You wait boys?" They both made for one of the curtains.

Doc rose like a cat so as to put himself in line with the gap as they swung the curtain aside. Then he lurched past, as though drunkenly seeking a lavatory. When the curtain was back in place he came back to Christy.

"Just as I thought. That was bloody cow-eyed Albert in there. They've gone to report to him. He's running them two. If there's anything I hate," he said baring his teeth, "it's a bludger. I think I'll do him over."

"You'll do nothing of the kind. He wants those two to pump us. Did you see the way the little shyte registered when you pretended to let something slip? No, Doc, this is the dinkum thing. I feel it in my bones. We get taken in by Ayoub Fanous and his two ladies."

"You're right, you old bastard. This is it, as the Poms say. Anyway, that Juliet's a tasty slice of stuff. What d'you reckon they're talking about back there?"

"Gloria asked me if we wanted to stay with them the rest of our leave. I said yes. They've gone to tell the unspeakable Albert we are hooked. Albert is the sort of man who deals in a hundred little things: drugs, prostitutes, and picking up information to sell to some contact. Just now, with a battlefront not very far away, information is commanding a good price; perhaps better than women or *hashish*. The agents have descended on Cairo and Alex."

"You know," mused Doc, "those posters we used to have up on the walls of canteens about THE ENEMY LISTENS, they don't sound like bull now, do they? It goes on, mate, it goes on."

"Your perception is uncanny."

"Why don't they just run bastards like Albert in and put 'em up against a wall?"

"Because the higher-ups would still be there and they could find a dozen more Alberts tomorrow. What we spill will go back down a long line. It will be put alongside what they've observed back in the field; and there they'll be putting on some sort of show that will fit in with what they learn this end. Then the trap's baited."

"You ought to have been a bloody general."

"I've often thought the same."

"Here they come back. Start looking silly again."

The girls advanced with a decisive and cheerful air.

"Makes you sick, don't it?" said Doc. "I'll get my money's worth out of her," he added viciously. "She'll know she'd had a man by the time I've finished with her."

The girls reseated themselves. Juliet acted as spokeswoman:

"We very much like you come with us until your leave stops.

Gloria and I live near each other so you two friends will not be far away."

"Now ain't that marvellous!" cried Doc rapturously.

"Heaven could provide no more," hiccuped Christy. He placed an unsteady arm about Gloria's bare shoulder and she made her eyes flare at him. Doc and Juliet were already looking at each other as though besotted. Christy rather thought Juliet would be a different woman by the morning. Doc had never looked more rapacious. They looked up to find a bearded man in a *gabaliyeh* holding out a small box. He addressed the men:

"Spanish Fly. Make you want woman, make woman want you. Make great lover. Make the big *zigazag*. Five hundred *piasters*."

"Are you," inquired Christy loftily, "casting doubts on our virility?"

"Fog off," Doc told the salesman. "I don't need no Spanish Fly." He hooted with mirth. "It'd only slow me down."

Juliet fawned on him and ran her gleaming lips about his face:

"No, you not need Spanish Fly. You are a big bronze Anzac."

"That's right!" boasted Doc, hiding her tiny waist beneath his hands. "A big bronze Anzac!"

Juliet turned and said something swift and insulting to the Arab, which caused him to mutter between white teeth and stalk off.

There was a crash and a scream from across the way. The big lesbian had come in and caught her "wife" with another. The outraged "husband" thrust the faithless one bodily up the stairs, with cheerful urging from the other patrons: the street-walkers, the dope-sellers, the pansies, and those of conventional appetites.

Suddenly Albert was with them again, as if he had sensed they were about to depart.

"Has everything been satisfactory, soldiers?"

"Like the bloody Hotel Australia," Doc told him, and rose, dragging Juliet with him.

"There is some money to pay, soldiers."

Doc eyed him dangerously.

"What for?" he asked softly.

Albert's eyes gazed an immortal innocence:

"Why, the drinks, Sergeant. As for the girls, that is their affair, you understand?"

Christy thrust some notes into Albert's hand and pushed him gently away. Albert bowed and went.

"Here!" called Doc, and threw him a hundred-piastre piece. "Something for the plate at church."

"You knew I go to church?" murmured Albert. "Clever soldier."

He melted once more into his curtain.

"Little bludger'll take his cut from them later," Doc was muttering.

"Anybody would think it was your own money you were spending," Christy told him.

• • • • •

Gloria and Juliet lived in rooms in an old street of tall stone, uncommunicative houses.

"This is my room," Juliet imparted, pointing up to a narrow balcony three flights above them some gaudy washing hung. "Come, Anzac, we will say good night."

For answer Doc picked up her small body and carried her through the entrance without a word.

"I am a short way along," Gloria told Christy. She smiled at him and added, "You will like it. It is clean and I do good cooking, learnt from my mother."

He smiled back. She is really rather pretty, he thought.

30

Over the wicked city of Cairo, called by some the wickedest in the world, the stars shone splendidly, in glittering torrents above the citizens; some of whom snored and some sinned, some made love and others bought it. And everything was for sale. Even unto the dawn hours drugs, bodies, and souls were being bought and enjoyed.

A hundred miles or so away the war also proceeded.

• • • • •

Christy and Gloria lay unclothed in bed together. She was very garrulous and had shown no coquetry, having explained that she had to like a man before she submitted, and would tell "Bill" of her life, after which they would be friends and so make love all night, and she would forget her sadness, her great sadness.

• • • • •

"I think the Germans will win the war," Juliet told Doc tauntingly.

Doc almost retorted: "Why, because you're helping them?" Instead, he yawned and said:

"Just as the moment I don't *care* who wins the war. Come here."

"Why?" she asked. She wore a transparent nightdress and her expression was mocking and shrewd. "You tell me who will win the war."

"We will," said Doc. "Just you read the newspapers next month."

"Why next month?"

"Never mind," said Doc, and sprang. He caught a handful of nightdress and tore it from her. Giggling, she pretended at first to resist, then to be overcome by his lusting.

• • • • •

"My mother was French," said Gloria, "my father was Lebanese. He was a merchant in Beirut."

"I thought you were French," remarked Christy.

"My father was arrested by the Australians after the fighting in Syria——"

"A Vichyite?"

"So one says. You were with the Australians fighting in Syria?"

"No, I was liberating Libya then."

"My mother died of malaria. There was little money and I became the mistress of an Australian officer. When he left Tripoli to go to Alamein I followed him here—but he was killed very soon in the fighting. Then I am very, as you say, hard-up. One night I meet Albert and he says 'You come and be hostess in the Mareka, get men to buy drinks and take commission and maybe find a nice man to keep you."

"No nice men yet?"

"You are nice," she said.

"Thank you!"

"Now we are friends," she said, and drew him to her. "You like my body?"

"I like your body. Your body is liked by me."

"You are crazy," she breathed at his ear.

• • • • •

"I know about men like you," Juliet told Doc. "You think only one thing about women. You like to hurt them, like you hurt me just now. You like to make them cry and say 'Do again please'—then you feel big bronze Anzac. You liked tearing my nightdress."

"You liked every minute of it," Doc said.

She giggled sinfully.

"You are very good soldier, I think. You kill many Germans?"

"Dozens of the bastards."

"Soon you fight them again, you say?"

"Did I?"

"Yes, I think I hear you say."

Doc lay and grinned at her evilly.

"You must have been mistaken. Anyhow, who cares about the war?"

She reverted to prurience. Her ear-rings jangled as she bent over him.

"You said right. I liked what you did."

"Got any more nightdresses?"

• • • • •

"You like me?" asked Gloria.

"Very much."

The round features were quite pretty and the body very nubile.

"It is very nice for some people to have liking in war. People have to do things they do not want to do all the time. My poor father did not want to work for Vichy people. I do not want to go to the Mareka. I do many things I do not want. It is very sad."

"You mean me?"

"No, no!" she said passionately. "I like you. I will let you stay without paying money."

Her breasts heaved upward, and he found her suddenly kneeling.

"If I tell you something——"

He pulled her up violently and jammed his lips on hers. He began to shake her from side to side.

"You are so passionate," she whispered after a minute.

My God, that was a close one, he thought.

31

THEY had Juliet's balcony room to themselves. They had sent the girls shopping, having developed a wish for home cooking. The room was cool and dim. The french windows stood wide open to reveal the building opposite and a festoon of washing.

"She kept trying to get me to spill my guts last night," Doc was saying. "I gave the bitch something else to think about."

"You were more fortunate than I," Christy told him. "Mine had an attack of conscience and tried to confess what she was up to on Albert's behalf. I stopped her just in time. Under the circumstances, I refrained from being indiscreet."

"I could have hit that slut last night, taking me for a mug like she was."

"What were you taking her for?"

"Don't worry, I'll get my money's worth out of her before I tell her what she wants." He suddenly broke into mirth. "The funny thing is, each of them will be learning the same thing. Albert could have halved his costs, if he only knew it."

"I'm a bit sorry for Gloria. She's at least doing her bit a little unwillingly."

"Well, mine can make love like a wild-cat—that's *my* consolation."

"Let's go to Gezira," said Christy, "and swim. After this feed they're going to give us."

"Take them?"

"Not on your life. I want to wash my sins away and forget them for an hour or two."

"And back to the Mareka tonight."

"That will be necessary, I should think. In any case, I'm looking forward to observing a little more life there."

. . . . .

At the Mareka that night Christy became an identity; a confessor, a benevolent president at a corner table. Early, he began to see it through a gentle haze, but that seemed the way in which to see it. He was not quite certain afterwards how it all began; but he did remember finding himself alone. Doc had gone off prowling somewhere on his own; Gloria and Julie were sitting with two drunken British soldiers whom they tricked and flattered into buying drink after drink.

His memory declared it to begin with his restoring peace between the lesbians.

"She cannot be trusted," the gross woman told him with a tear beginning grotesquely in her eye, pointing at the other. She could speak no English and therefore had no chance to defend herself. But the look on Christy's face caused the lips to quiver harder than ever, and through the gross woman she said:

"Your eyes are kind. You do not despise us. Our problems are as real to us as ordinary people."

"You are both people with problems," he told the gross woman. "She is weak. You should protect her."

At which the gross woman burst into tears too, embraced the other, vowing eternal gratitude to Christy, who to tell the truth wondered what he *had* done. They left with arms around each other.

His next memory was of discussing Mozart with the pansy. After that he was the centre of a circle at his table; Greek, Egyptian, Palestinian sat around as though he were some kind of sage, and those who did not understand what he said demanded to be told.

Then, quite clearly, there was Gloria sitting alone with him, crying.

"They like you, Beel. They know you do not think them bad people. You are drunk and you make jokes against them, but they think you have helped them."

"Me? I merely got into conversation with them."

"You let them tell you about themselves. No people do that for *them*. You perhaps let *me* tell you all about myself?"

Here it is again, he thought.

"I am too drunk," he told her. "I can hardly understand what you are saying. Take me home."

"Yes! I will take you home. The British soldiers I leave. They have not money to ask to come home with me, so instead they make dirty words they think I do not understand. That is their sex thrill. Poof!"

She helped him up and drew his arms about her shoulder.
"I look after you," she told him tenderly.

32

WHICH she did. As soon as they got to her room he pretended to collapse on the bed. He endured being undressed and put between the covers. Then he actually did pass out.

In the morning she brought him breakfast, handing him the tray with a quaint air of respect. She sat on the edge of the bed and looked at him searchingly.

"You are well?" she asked.

He clapped a hand to his head.

"I feel very sick," he lied.

"You must stay in bed today," she said firmly. "I will look after you."

I'm going to be far too ill to listen to you unburden your soul, he thought. He lay back and groaned.

She laid a hand on his brow.

"Oh, my poor Beel!"

This is ludicrous! he told himself. He groaned again.

She drew her robe aside and laid his head against a bare breast.

"I will look after you," she repeated.

I'll yell with laughter in a minute!

He groaned yet a third time and buried his face in the pillow.

He fell asleep again. When he awoke he found Doc's face grinning at him satanically from the end of the bed.

"How's poor Beel?"

"Get fogged," snarled Christy.

"What's the strong of this? You look all right to me."

"I have got a bit of a hang-over, but nothing worse than usual. I'm dead scared that girl's going to spill her guts to me. That could put everything up to poop bonzer."

Doc began to rock with laughter and Christy eyed him sourly.

"I hear you were the star turn at the Mareka last night."

"Where were you last night, coot?"

"Someone has to attend to details," replied Doc, self-righteously. "I went to the hotel, collected the rest of our gear, and settled the bill."

"And spent the night with Esmeralda."

"Maybe."

"Has Juliet managed to worm the vital information out of you yet?"

Doc grinned diabolically.

"Not yet."

"Where's Gloria gone?"

"Out, to get medicine for you I suppose."

Christy rose. "Let's get out of here before she gets back. I'll leave a note for her. Come on!"

As they were going down the stairs Doc said:

"Do you realise we've only got three days?"

. . . . .

Christy was in the Mareka again that night, at the same table. As the *habitués* arrived they came over to pay their respects. Perhaps at last, he thought wryly, I have found my true role: counsellor and comforter of the despised and the depraved.

Both he and Doc took their women home early. Albert drifting wide-eyed in and out of curtains, offered no objection. Business was obviously good.

. . . . .

The stars shone down.

"Australians are best soldiers in the world," Juliet said fawningly. "They will best the Germans."

"Bloody oath we will," Doc told her. "Wait till next month."

"What part of next month?"

Doc didn't answer.

. . . . .

"Whatever you have done that is wrong," Christy was saying, "don't tell me, I don't care. I forgive you in the name of whoever you have done wrong."

"Even if it is you I have done wrong?"

"I have done you far more than you have possibly done me. I have bought from you what should be yielded only in love and affection."

"But I give it to you with affection," she said passionately. "I will take no money from you."

"That's stupid."

"No, I have a reason. It is, what you say, ato——at——"

"Atonement?"

"Yes."

"And the affection?"

"I give you that too. I think you are a wise, good man."

If you only knew, thought Christy.

33

IT was Sunday. Previously, Albert had come up to Christy and said:

"Mr. Bill, you have made here quite a hit. We are all bad people but we like you. In the corner there you sit, quiet with the drink, and people bring to you their hopeless cases, as though you are—I do not know how to say. A man who listens and judges and says: 'It is all right, I know of worse.' Ayoub Fanous is perhaps the most of the hopeless cases, but he has one virtue——"

Here Albert drew the weight of his eyes heavenwards. His face glistened with emotion. "—I still, every Sunday, go to the Coptic Church in the Old City."

"Most commendable," murmured Christy, feeling both revolted and amused.

"It would do me the greatest honour," proceeded Albert, "if the next Sunday you should accompany me to the service in the morning."

The invitation appealed to Christy at once. The thought of attending divine worship with the most noxious little creature he had ever encountered was an experience not to be passed over. That such a creature, knowing that Christy knew of him (not to mention the secret knowledge) should so earnestly try to evince a remnant of what he called "virtue", did not touch Christy in the least. It increased his contempt. But it appealed to his sense of the macabre. In future years, or even when he rejoined the Fifty-Fifth and talked with Kirk and Pascoe, he imagined himself describing Albert's nature and activities, and capping it all by telling them how he accompanied Albert to a Coptic Church for the purpose of worshipping God. Yes, it was far too good to be missed.

So he gravely accepted, and it was only then that Albert informed him that the mass began at half past six in the morning. Would Bill meet him at six, so they could take a tram out to the old city? Still gravely, he agreed.

Like any old infantryman, he could wake himself at will. He did so this Sunday at half past five. Bathed, shaved, dressed, he met Albert dead on time.

Albert wore a suit of black alpaca, a white shirt, and a black tie. On his head was a black hat. He seemed craven, guilty, withdrawn. He reminded Christy of a defrocked priest.

As he came up to Albert, Christy noted that he was shaven clean instead of covered in his usual sweat-beaded stubble. Albert took off his hat and shook hands. Solemnly Christy responded.

"We will walk to the tram," said Albert, as though they were already in the confines of a church.

Christy nodded. He let Albert make all the conversation as they walked. One of the reasons for his taciturnity was his enjoyment of this Sabbath Albert; the other was that as soon as he had emerged into the fresh air this morning he found himself to be suffering from a villainous hangover. His head throbbed and the pavement jumped before his eyes.

To add to his suffering, the tram was jammed with citizens of Cairo in all their garbs and odours. As he entered, they seemed to Christy to be oozing from the windows. He wondered why there were so many so early in the morning, and whether they were all Christians bound for church. The journey seemed interminable. He told himself that the tram was stopping at lamp-posts as well as tram stops. More and more people got on but only a few got off and these always appeared to be fat men in the very middle of the tram whose vociferous passage to the exit made his head hammer harder than ever. He was sure that only the bodies jammed against him on all sides held him upright.

All the time Albert kept his eyes demurely lowered. Even his thick round lips had taken on a severe set, as though he were already in spirit with the solemnities before them. Held up between hot, heaving bodies, his clangorous head like a block of iron on his shoulders, Christy closed his eyes and dimly heard Albert saying:

"This church where I take you is seven hundred years old. In the crypt is the place where Saint Sentius was martyred."

Christy nodded. I know just how martyrs feel, he was thinking.

The journey seemed to go on and on. Strange tongues spoke around him, the tramcar clattered and clanged, bodies pressed the breath out of him. The left side of his head was meeting the right side in the middle with a thump-thump-thump. Then they parted and the brain fell back with a crash into its proper place.

Suddenly Albert's voice said:

"We are here."

Christy heaved against a solid wall of flesh which finally yielded and let him through. Still thrusting, he reached the exit and made solid earth once again. He opened his eyes fully to the morning.

The Old City gloomed back at him. Domes and minarets and high latticed walls. Twisting streets with deep backwaters of shade. Arabia without its perfumes.

Albert led him decorously to the church. They entered a doorway in a high grey stone wall and so into a dim and musty atmosphere. Christy was grateful for the dimness, if nothing else. But his ordeal soon began.

For the ceremony lasted four hours, and nobody sat. The officiating priest, a black-robed, black-bearded, Christ-like man intoned endlessly, and after him came various members of the congregation, who came to read in a wailing sing-song from the bible, in Hebrew or Arabic—or was it some other language? Christy could not afterwards remember many of Albert's whispered explanations. All he gained in the way of impressions was the doleful intonations of the readers and the heavy smell of tapers.

If he could only sit down! But no one else did. What were the bloody seats for then? People came in, stayed to read, then departed, but not Albert. Eventually Albert came forward to read, and acquitted himself as wailingly and incomprehensibly as any of the others. Christy had a sense of agonised timelessness.

Then the priest came along the congregation and dispensed holy water at a range of a yard from each recipient, and Christy realised with grateful joy that it was over at last.

They walked back out into the bright sunlight, against which Christy had to half-close his aching eyes.

"It was interesting, was it not?" Albert asked him sanctimoniously.

"Oh, yes!" groaned Christy.

"I am uplifted by it," said Albert, "even though I am Fallen."

Christy fought strongly with a desire to deal Albert a running kick in the behind.

34

HE found Doc at the café where they had arranged to meet. There was a beer ready waiting for him, for Doc had seen him in the distance. Christy downed it wolfishly, then leaned back with a shudder.

"I never knew you was religious," Doc said curiously.

"Four hours it lasted," replied Christy faintly, "four mortal hours of hellish whining in strange languages, on and on like a gramophone record that never ends. And I never sat once. They've got stamina, these Copts. And the egregious Albert. Never shall I forget the sight of that little wretch almost hidden behind this huge tome, whining and wailing with the best of them. A quiet, pious, respectable citizen of Cairo! I had some wild desire to get up and tell all these brother Copts what he really was—until it occurred to me that perhaps some of them already knew. I realised I was in another man's world, among different minds——"

"Cool down," grunted Doc. "Have another beer."

"Well," Christy asked some minutes later, and in a much stronger voice, "how have we done?"

"Diddly-Dum'll be proud of us. We've struck oil here all right. I wonder if they'll ever do anything about Albert and those girls."

"When they've served their purpose."

"I dunno, it's all beyond me, this business of kidding each other up and letting spies run around loose. Give me a nice straight dose of action any day. It's cleaner."

"Have you split your guts to Juliet yet?" Christy wanted to know.

"I'm giving her the lot tonight. How about you?"

"I shall have to be subtle. Mine doesn't want to find out anything for the unspeakable Albert. She has attacks of remorse. She's not a bad girl, really. Yours—I think she has a streak of viciousness. She enjoys it."

Doc grinned. "So do I."

"Our last night in Cairo," mused Christy. "How shall we spend it?"

"Same as other nights, only more so."

• • • • •

Christy farewelled the *habitués* of the Mareka that night. Christy felt as though he had been coming to this place for a long time, not just a few days. He knew he would never come back, even if the opportunity should present itself. It was a scene in the grim comedy that Doc and he had come to play. Without the bizarre purpose in the background he felt it would be different, probably bore him. The amount of amusement to be had from these people in the Mareka was strictly limited. But tonight, his last of the leave, he was amiable. He welcomed the air of unreality that grew around him.

Albert was softly attentive. "Many soldiers come to the Mareka, Bill, and are soon forgotten. But I think we will remember you. You are like the other soldiers and yet you are quite different. People who are in here regularly will miss you. People who are not very good have pleasure in someone like you. Who shall sit in your chair now?"

You little humbug! Christy called him silently. Outwardly he acknowledged Albert's compliments with a slow nod of the head. Well, Albert would never know how he had served the Allied cause while believing himself to be doing the opposite. This was a rich joke, this double-game, this gulling of a sly little procurer—but he was beginning to tire of it.

They came to say good-bye to him on learning it was his last night: the lesbians, the pansy, the hashish-sellers, the prostitutes. He bought them all drinks, wondering just what quality—or failing—in him had attracted them. Perhaps, he thought, our instincts are basically similar. Have we all rejected a great part of life? Do they recognise in me something I don't even recognise in myself? His needs and desires were different from theirs, they would not understand most of the things that moved him to pain or anger or joy; and yet in him they had undoubtedly recognised something.

When he was sober he would give it some more thought. In the meantime, here was Gloria inclined towards seeing this parting tearfully and dramatically.

While assuring her she would recover from her present desolation, he kept an eye on Doc, who was arguing with Juliet. This being their last night, Doc might get it into his head to do anything, and their job was not quite over.

But Doc seemed determined to stay with Juliet. It was not only the job—something else, an antagonism, a resolve to get the utmost from her before he left her, was evident in his manner. Christy breathed a sigh of relief. All in all, Doc hadn't been too bad.

Around midnight he and Doc collected the two girls and left. They parted and said good night in the narrow street and Christy took a snivelling Gloria up the stairs.

"Now I want you to be gay," he said, feeling anything but. "No serious talk, and no more tears, please."

"You are very good, very kind," she sniffed. "I do not like most men I meet in the Mareka."

He patted her shoulder. "Wait till the war ends. Things will be better for you."

In the room she said to him:

"I am crying because you are going, but you should be crying. It is you who will soon be in danger and perhaps getting hurt."

"Yes," he agreed, nodding. "On the fourth of next month."

She gave another sob and hid herself against him. The face above her shoulder was grinning widely.

• • • • •

Doc's leave had reached a height of sadistic enjoyment. He lay next to Juliet, remembering each beer, each unidentified drink, each woman he had taken in those few days. The girl lay sleeping after a rough handling.

Corpus and I have to be at the station early. This morning, at the very last moment, I shall give her the rest of the information that little animal Albert has been on at her to get. He looked aside at the sharp, dusky features. The little sneak! The bloody little phoney! If only I could let her know that I'm not the fool she thinks me; that she's the one being taken for a ride. If only I could give her a bloody good hiding and tell her what it was all about. Bloody little Wog slut!

He fell into dreamless sleep. When he awoke, it was first light. He felt fresh and strong. He leaned over Juliet and began to fondle her. The grand finale!—he thought.

She awoke and murmured for the hundredth time how strong he was. He did not fail to notice the cunning expression on her face. She was going to get her information—but how she was going to pay!

"You are hurting me," she said, but there was pleasure in her voice.

"You must be a mass of bruises," he said; and grinned.

He felt the need to climax his association with her by something brutal and memorable. It was as though she could answer some cruel need in him. He needed her and hated her for making him need, for awakening an appetite beyond mere lust. He thought her frail body was going to break against him.

He closed his eyes against a sudden dizziness, and saw not darkness but exploding colours. His hand found her throat and his fingers began to kneed the soft flesh. She began to toss against him.

He gripped harder, for he felt that her throat alone connected him with solid matter and if he let go he would be lost up in some blank unknown. He heard her make sounds, strangely gratifying sounds.

Then the cold fact of what he was doing asserted itself, like a mechanism clicking into place. He forced his hands apart and withdrew them, at the same time opening his eyes.

"Yes, you are strong," she whispered hoarsely.

"Did I hurt you?" he asked, amazed to find he was breathing as if after a hard run.

"Yes," she answered, and the gleam in her eyes was not that of fear, but of some strange elation. Something in her answered him strongly, triumphantly.

Little Wog slut! She suited him, they were of a piece. If he ever came back to Cairo he would look her up—before anybody.

"I got carried away a bit," he admitted. "It was the idea of having to go back up the desert into the fighting."

She clung to him hard, saying soothingly:

"Have you to fight again so soon, my poor Doc?"

"Yes," he told her, and made his final payment. "The fourth of next month."

35

THE train rattled its way through the Nile valley, and Christy settled down with a sense of repletion. It was all over. They had drunk and whored and done their job. Albert, Juliet, and Gloria had come to the station to see them off. Albert was once more his ordinary self: the grubby suit, the long gross nose with the nostrils like two extra eyes, the masking lids, the thick red lips, and the air of unassuming evil. Juliet wore a scarf around her neck, and said good-bye to Doc with a look in her eye that suggested something strange between them, an exhilarating secret shared. And Gloria, dressed becomingly in a plain white dress, had eyes for none but Christy, looking up at him with an air that combined adoration and contrition.

"I thought Horrible might have come," Doc had remarked, looking round him.

"Too much risk," said Christy. "Too many provosts."

Time to get aboard. Albert had shaken their hands unctuously, Juliet had embraced Doc fiercely for the last time, Gloria had wept quietly against Christy and made him promise to see her next time he was in Cairo. Juliet had extracted no such promise from Doc, as if she knew that in future Doc would home to her when he returned to Cairo. She had an air of achievement. Doc just grinned at her.

Then the train was in motion, they were settling down and what Christy felt must be one of the strangest soldiers' leaves in the history of modern warfare was over.

They both closed their eyes and were silent for some minutes.

"Well," said Doc at last, "I wonder when the information will reach the Germans?"

"I should think," replied Christy, not bothering to open his eyes, "that may safely be left to Albert."

He began to whistle mournfully.

"I reckon we might get mentioned in dispatches for this caper," said Doc after another silence.

Christy shrugged moodily, still whistling. It occurred to him that if he ever got to Cairo again, Albert and those two girls would probably be behind bars. Then he laughed:

"You know, if ever Albert has to go out of business, the Mareka will be right up Horrible John's street."

"Old Horrible!"—Doc shook his head. "Yair, he'd go all right in the Mareka."

They had a compartment to themselves, and both lay at full length on the seat. Christy felt deflated. He was glad to see Cairo receding, but made sad by what lay ahead of him. Poor old Fifty-Fifth! He was beginning to see this leave as wholly degrading. Somewhere along the line he had lost that delicious sense of irony. He felt very tired, very old.

"Well," Doc went on, a gloating look on his face, "we've got a couple of secrets we can amuse ourselves with when we get back to the Fifty-Fifth. When we start this stink, for instance, we'll know we helped to make sure there was plenty of opposition. I wonder what they'd say if they knew. I doubt whether we'd be thanked."

"We'll be copping it too."

"Yes—we shall pay for our sins."

He began to whistle again, and Doc, looking irritated, asked him:

"What's that bloody tune you keep whistling?"
For answer, Christy began to sing it in a soft baritone:

The Minstrel Boy to the war is gone,
In the ranks of death you'll find him;
His father's sword he has girded on,
And his wild harp slung behind him.

METHOD

36

Colonel Kirk could feel the attack building up, the plan shaping itself, the elements taking their places ready for the explosion, the point of change. Last night a camouflage section had come up and erected dummy tanks on the flat behind the Fifty-Fifth's positions. Each night until the actual assault, the tanks would be moved, so that enemy reconnaissance should not suspect.

The men in the companies, though told nothing yet, had begun to murmur their suspicions. Now they were watching for every trivial sign to confirm them. Company commanders going daily to Battalion Headquarters for conferences, a sudden access to ammunition. The old hands could smell it in the air.

"Why do they always pick on us? Anybody'd think we were the only battalion in the A.I.F."

This was the refrain of the companies; partly bitter, partly proud. They bred 'em tough in the Numerella, and the bloody general knew it. There was going to be a show and it looked as though the Fifty-Fifth might be starring again. They weren't conscripts, they hadn't had to join up; there was nothing to do but soldier on. But fog the army, fog the general, fog old Diddly-Dum, anyway!

Patrol activity was stepped up, always a sure sign of something in the offing. Kirk was encouraged by the reports from patrols. The Hun seemed to be taking the bait. Patrols had found new observation posts, reinforced positions, and a far hotter reception for penetrating patrols. The AILO had reported that aerial reconnaissance photos showed enemy tanks moving up.

Ted had come over in a jeep one day, to see him. The burning of the sun had concealed the new lines around his eyes, but the boy's whole bearing, the look in his eyes, even the set of his shoulders were those of a man suddenly very much older, very much more aware of the meaning of life. He was both subdued and strengthened by the knowledge of how expendable life was on this battleground. The Colonel knew that he was talking now to an equal in experience and skill. He tried to show nothing of the parent in his manner, and was awkward and preoccupied. He kept the talk on to the immediate, they mentioned Freda Kirk and Numerella only in passing.

When Ted left, Kirk walked to his jeep with him. This was the awkwardest moment of all.

"Keep your head down, son."

They shook hands, and Ted stood back and saluted. The Colonel responded, and stood watching the jeep dissolve in a cloud of dust. He descended to the Battalion Orderly dug-out, and stood a few moments while his eyes adjusted themselves to the shade; then walked through and sat at his own table. He was sitting there staring silently at the boards, his head between his hands, when Stainforth came in, and said, "Excuse me, sir, there's a signal."

The Colonel raised his head and straightened himself.

"Yes," he said slowly. "Let's have it."

• • • • •

Pascoe was listening to some of his men talking in a near-by *doover*. It was early evening, just after the stand-to. For once, there was no patrol tonight. Pascoe missed Christy and their nightly arguments. No amount of talk with the rest of the company took their place; nobody but Christy could convince him that life was not entirely senseless and unanswerable. What was Christy really? A pessimist or an optimist? A pessimist, perhaps, in his attitudes, an optimist in his acts, which had compassion and dignity.

"So old Herbie Drummond got off?" remarked a voice.

"Well, he was innocent."

"Like hell he was. He helped Horrible get away, all right."

"Yair, but they can't prove it."

"Look, I heard it from Stan Pollock, who was in the orderly room when Herbie was hauled up."

"What happened?"

"Well, Diddly-Dum asks Herbie what he knew about Horrible John getting away. Herbie just gazes at him innocent-like and says: 'Same as I told the provosts, sir. I go round the back to the latrines and when I get back Horrible's disappeared, and so's me hat and me belt.' Diddly-dum didn't muck around trying to trip Herbie up. Once Herbie's settled on his story, a grenade couldn't shake him. So he just grins a bit and tells Herbie he's to be cook's offsider at Battalion for a week, and to report to Bastable in full kit for an hour's pack drill every afternoon. Herbie knows better than to argue about that, and as he's going out, Diddly-Dum calls him back and says: 'Incidentally, Private Drummond, the whole business was extremely well planned. It shows evidence of a good military mind.' 'Thank you, sir,' says Herbie."

After their laughter died away, another voice said reminiscently:

"Old Herbie's never stuck for an answer. Do you remember the time he over-stayed his leave three days in Tel Aviv?"

"Which time was this?"

"Well, Herbie was about fourteenth to be paraded for Ack Willie this morning, and Diddly-Dum was getting tired of all the old excuses being dished up to him, so when Herbie comes in Diddly-Dum says: 'And what's your story, Private Drummond.

Were you taken ill and unable to travel? Did you lose your pay-book and go looking for it? Or did you just misread the date on your leave pass?' "

" 'Sir,' says Herbie, 'I cannot tell a lie——'

" 'Not much you can't,' says Diddly-Dum, 'but go on, I'm interested.'

" 'Well, sir,' says Herbie, 'you know I'm a keen poker player, don't you? Well, I get into a big poker school in Tel Aviv, composed almost entirely of mugs who've got plenty of money to lose. It takes me three days to soften them up, 'cos you can't take it off 'em too sudden, or they pack up. I needed them three extra days to complete the job. It was a golden opportunity, sir, and I just couldn't give it a miss. So I reckoned on what I might get fined for the Ack Willy, and what I was going to take off these mugs, and I decided it was worth it. So here I am.'

" 'I'm a very keen poker player myself,' says Diddly-Dum. 'How much did you win?'

" 'About seventy quid,' Herbie tells him.

" 'So,' says Diddly-Dum fingering his chin—you know how he does it—'you don't expect to bring as much as seventy quid, Private Drummond?'

" 'Why, no, sir,' says Herbie aghast.

" 'Tell me, Private Drummond, you as a man accustomed to weighing the odds for and against the winning chances of certain combinations of cards and bidding accordingly, what would be your bid for three days' A.W.L.?'

" 'Two quid,' says Herbie like a flash.

" 'Five quid,' says the Colonel just as quickly.

" 'I'll see yer,' says Herbie.

"Well, Herbie had called his hand, so the Colonel had to let him off with a fiver fine. Yes, he's smart, old Herbie."

"He didn't *have* to let Herbie off with a fiver," another voice objected. "It's just his form."

"Have you ever heard him and Corpus having a tussle? Gawd, it's a classic!"

"I don't know how Corpus gets away with it, fair dinkum."

"Corpus is a bloody genius, that's how."

"Didn't him and Diddly work together before the war?"

"Not together exactly. Diddly's a District Inspector and Corpus's just an employee in the Inspection Branch, under him, like."

"I wonder what those two bastards are up to in Cairo?"

"I'll tell you. Doc'll be flat out on top of a sheila and Corpus'll be poking round some place that's strictly out of bounds talking to queer types. He collects 'em."

"He's a queer type himself."

"He's the sanest man you'll ever meet," said Pascoe approaching.

"You been earwigging, Boss?"

"Yes."

"Just as well we weren't talking about you, wasn't it?"

37

"THOSE two are back, sir," Sergeant Bastable told the Colonel.

"Do you mean Sergeant Home and Private Christy?"

"Yes, sir."

"Well, refer to them by their rank."

"Yes, sir. Sergeant Home and Private Christy have reported back from leave, sir."

"You sound surprised. Send 'em in."

The Colonel composed himself against the sandy wall of his dug-out. Outside, he could hear Bastable's hectoring tones being answered by the nasal acidity of Doc Home. He supposed that in a few minutes he would know whether the decision of Intelligence to send two non-officers on this particular mission had been a sound one. Intelligence probably knew the German mind better than he did. The idea that no German intelligence man could believe in two officers being so irresponsible as to blab the date of an important action sounded valid enough—but Kirk was harried by doubts. He doubted almost everything concerned with the pending attack. It was too tortuous to be militarily sound; there were too many trivial details which held success at their mercy.

They came stooping into the dug-out, stood at attention in front of him; Doc said "Up!" and they both saluted. The Colonel gave a nod of acknowledgement.

"Take a seat," he told them. "Now I want the opinion of both of you and want it in cold blood. Forget how you feel. I've got to send a report back to Corps as to whether this information has been leaked successfully. You understand? So tell me how you both went in plain, cold English."

Christy and Doc looked at each other. Recollection passed between them; they broke slowly into grins. Kirk found himself grinning too. He had a deep line on either side of his face, which ran from cheekbone to chin, and it folded in humorously as he watched them.

"I can see you've had the time of your lives."

Doc assured him this was so.

"Well, sir," he began, "Corpus and I talked it over coming back, and we're morally certain that the info is well and truly on its way."

He began to report, referring occasionally to Christy. His grin gone, the Colonel listened.

• • • • •

Three-quarters of an hour later, Christy and Doc emerged into the Battalion Orderly Room, where they were met by Price-Gore.

"Would you chaps let me have your leave passes please."

"Whay, certainly, old chappay!" Doc told him, in an outrageous mimicry of Price-Gore's tones. "Heah we are, and you jolly well know what you can do with it, what?"

Blushing a little, Price-Gore took their leave passes. He had been persecuted too long by Doc to offer any rebuke. At first, he had put Doc's mockery down to an attempt to mask a feeling of inferiority. Doc was a vulgar, uneducated fellow, and was best ignored. Then Price-Gore had realised that what Doc felt for him was an amused contempt. He thought Price-Gore funny, from his neat little moustache to the mirror-like toes of his boots.

Doc's attention was suddenly caught by the right arm of Price-Gore's shirt. He came closer and peered.

"Oh, no!" he cried. 'Look, Corpus, it's got a third stripe. I'm reverting to the ranks. I'm not going to share the sergeants' mess with rabbit-head here."

"The prospect of sharing——" began Price-Gore primly.

"Let's get out of here," interrupted Christy, handing his leave pass over. "Congratulations, Pricey. You'll bring the necessary tone to the snake-pit; something it badly needs. Come on, Doc."

"Toodle-oo, Pricey Wicey," called Doc, and followed Christy out into the open. He looked around for Bastable, in order to deal his old enemy some further abuse, but Bastable had gone to earth somewhere. Still grumbling about having to share the sergeants' mess with "that pansified little Pommy poon", he made for the transport lines to get a truck to Don Company.

"How does Cairo seem to you now?" asked Christy as they lay in the back of a *ute*. "Like a riotous dream, so vivid it was almost real?"

"It was real all right," grinned Doc. "Boy, was it real!"

"So's this," said Christy pointing out to the dust that boiled up behind the truck, to the flat stones, like mirrors to the dazzling sun. There was gun-fire in the distance.

"Yair," Doc agreed reflectively. He lay swaying to the movements of the *ute*, staring out at the desert which for a few days he had entirely forgotten. "You know," he burst out at last, sitting upright and slapping his bare knee, "this caper, this whole bloody idea, couldn't be any madder than if the bloody army was commanded by a lunatic, and we were all stark staring mad and were just trying to find out the most complicated way of getting ourselves massacred."

Christy did not reply. He seemed to be asleep, but he was thinking that in a rough way Doc had just summarised war itself.

38

THE men of Don Company speculated daily over what was in store for them. Every small new sign was noted and discussed. An armourer came up and went over their weapons; Pascoe's ammunition store was piled with boxes. That German reconnaissance plane seemed to be spending much of its time above their part of the front.

As they talked Doc and Christy listened and often exchanged a glance. They were, of course, the centre of all talk for several days, having newly returned from leave in Cairo; and Doc needed no urging to relate certain of his exploits, both with drink and women. With any other man they would have suspected exaggeration. But they knew their Doc. The old hands who had accompanied him on leaves had envied and admired his ruthless preying after bodily pleasure. They believed every wild, sordid tale he told them.

Doc and Christy had brought several bottles of drink back with them. These were distributed among the Company to loud thanks. It tended to abate the envious abuse with which the two returning leave-takers were greeted.

As the days passed, Doc became all warrior. Sixteen Platoon began to feel the rough edge of his tongue; only Christy remained impervious to his harshness. Sixteen Platoon having no officer at the moment, Doc was commander, and made them know it.

"If I ever see that bloody rifle as dirty as that again," he told Private Ryman, "I'll bash it over your head. That's your best friend, that smoke-pole, in case you don't know it."

"Who told you to let off that safety-catch?" he snarled at Private Watford during a stand-to one night. "That's how accidents happen."

He went along the trench muttering something about dopey-looking bastards of reos.

Farther down he discovered Christy, instead of standing-to, kneeling down patting the dog.

"You're in this war too, sport," he said.

"Are we in danger of imminent attack?" Christy inquired.

"*You* are," Doc told him bitterly.

"Simmer down," said Christy. "You're as nervous as a cat."

"So would you be in my shoes. I'm trying to get these reos into some sort of order. I hope they don't take you as a model."

He prodded the dog with the toe of his boot, and asked:

"What are you doing with this miserable thing when we go in?"

"Same as last time. Send it back to Battalion."

Doc looked around him, then joined Christy as he squatted.

"I only hope," he said very softly, "that I don't get some snotty-nosed little loot, fresh from Duntroon, at the very last minute. That'd be the stone bloody end."

"I think," Christy told him, "that Vik Kirk, being right out of officers, will probably leave Sixteen Platoon in your tender care . . . poor bastards," he added.

"They're safer with me than some pink-cheeked, hairy-arsed boy from an officers' school."

"Personally, I can't see them being too safe with anyone," observed Christy.

Doc looked glumly up at the brilliant stars.

"No," he agreed; and sighed.

There was a curious numbness in Christy's mind. He neither dreaded nor anticipated this impending action. As a poet, too, he had for the moment dried up. He supposed the reason was that he knew all about it, had long ago exhausted the emotional processes: the irony, the coming to terms with possible death, the wondering whether life had been worth it. I'm getting old, he thought. There's too much sadness under the sun.

A chill came over the earth. In the west the sky glowed with the first touch of the moon above the black ridges. A Very light soared and burst high in the heavens, and as it fell lit a circle of desert, as though a searchlight had found for an instant the face of a strange planet. The stars were still, and intense.

Christy lay out on the sand with a blanket over him, the dog lying close to his body, the thin nose buried against his master. Presently Pascoe loomed up beside them and, throwing a groundsheet next to Christy, lowered himself down, pulling a greatcoat about him.

"You know what's going to happen, don't you?" he demanded.

"I have my suspicions," said Christy sleepily.

"Every man in this company knows damned well we're going into action in the very near future. Don't ask me when, because I haven't been told. I've just been staring at maps and sand-tables."

This is unique, thought Christy: a company commander confessing he did not know the date of an attack to a private who knew the date, the plan, and all that had gone on before. Oh, war, you amusing creature!

"Oh, I know the day we're attacking," said Christy blithely.

Pascoe grunted unappreciatively, and in the darkness Christy grinned.

"The dog knows too," Christy added. "He can sense it all. He dreams."

"So do I. Do you?"

"Sometimes."

"What of?"

"Oh, of trees, and lost opportunities, and girls I might have had, poems I nearly wrote, people I should have killed, and people I ought to have loved."

"I have an awful, nameless sort of dream, and after it I wake up longing for a dose of action, acting like a purgative on a mind constipated with useless questions. I dream sometimes of doing violent, magnificent, unthought things, such as a leopard or an eagle do."

"H'm . . . We play a deathly game, to rules drawn up by ourselves, while the beast of prey plays it to rules he isn't even aware of, let alone questions."

"Don't you envy men like Doc Home sometimes?" asked Pascoe.

"Yes. Only a few days ago in Cairo."

"Did you do anything at all interesting there, or did you just trail around drinking and whoring with Doc?"

"One or two interesting things. I promise to tell you about them after this stink is over."

"Why wait?"

"I have my reasons. I'll tell you when it's over."

The unspoken thought hovered between them like a bird of the night.

39

"SLOPE arms!" barked Sergeant Bastable.

He was giving Private Drummond his pack drill on a piece of flat ground near Battalion Headquarters. Private Drummond, known as Doggy, appeared to consider the order for a minute, as he stood there laden with full pack, draped with webbing equipment, bayonet fixed. He raised his unlovely features to the sky, then seemed to have made up his mind.

"I said *Slope arms*!" roared Bastable.

Drummond contemplatively took the pack from his back and dropped it. He stuck his rifle in the sand by the bayonet. He drew forth from his pocket the makings of a smoke, then lowered himself on the ground and settled back to roll a cigarette.

"ON . . . YOUR . . . FEET!" thundered Bastable, his eyes almost prodding out of his head.

Drummond went on rolling his cigarette. Bastable strode up like a bull looking for a matador to gore.

"You're under arrest!"

"I already am."

"I mean close arrest."

"Bastable," said Drummond, licking the cigarette paper, then poking the tobacco in with a matchstick at the ends, "don't ever go up a dark lane with me after the war, 'cos only me'll come out the other end."

Bastable swallowed and suppressed an urge to kick the reclining private on to his feet.

"And where," he asked, "do you think this will get you? You'll only get extra pack drill. On your feet and do it like a man."

"I wonder how the old Horrible's doing?" Doggy mused wistfully. "You know, Bastable, you're talking to a military genius—Diddly-Dum admits it after the way I helped old Horrible. Now, I've studied the situation. We're going into a stink in the very near future, and I want to be with me mates, not listening to you scream at me. So I'm on strike, see? You can do what you like about it."

"You wait here," snarled Bastable.

"I ain't doin' anything special," drawled Doggy.

The incident eventually reached the attention of the Colonel. He sent for Bastable who, inwardly trembling, told Kirk all that had occurred. Trying to hide a grin, Kirk considered for a minute. Then:

"Send him back to his company," he said. "We'll settle this particular battle later. He's a good soldier."

. . . . .

"I tell yers, they're fattening us for the kill," Private Ryman was observing to the others of his section. "Every night now they come up with hot stew and spuds and old Puckerlips has just pulled up at Company. I'll bet yers he's got a lot of comforts aboard."

The Padre indeed did. The men came up from the shade of their *doovers* into the sun, and the Padre distributed the comforts. Toothpaste, chewing-gum, socks, chocolate, and twenty cigarettes. Trading began almost immediately, the non-smokers striking the most successful bargains with their cigarettes.

"It's a waste, giving them toothpaste," Pascoe told the Padre as they stood watching the men wander back to their *doovers*. "Most of them use their toothbrushes to clean their weapons with."

"Oh, they can rinse their mouths out with it."

Some of them, perhaps many, will soon be dead, blinded, mutilated, thought the Padre. They know it. What can I do to comfort them? If I let them know how I felt for them they would shun me. In the entire battalion, there are no more than five whom I can comfort with the thought of God. I don't suppose many of them believe in God. Those who do would rather not have Him talked about. Most of them think privately that there's not much God can do about all this. It was at the mercy of chance. They were all fatalists. If the bullet had your name on it, there was nothing you could do. It would find you. You just accepted what happened. Indeed we are underlings! thought the Padre. And yet the selfsame underlings could tower in their heroism and never give it a thought.

He watched Christy as he strolled across the stones towards him, his long figure relaxed, a tear in his yellow shorts, no buttons on his shirt which hung aside to reveal a brown, bony chest, tin hat well back on the grizzled hair, socks falling over the tops of the sanded-white boots, gun slung at his shoulder. He can give them more comfort than me! the Padre told himself. I suppose I lack the common touch. To these men, living amidst death and always next to each other, always depending on each other, nailed together by necessity, the common touch was valued above all else. And I haven't got it. I would not even know how to start getting it.

Like the rest of the battalion, he knew about Christy's acts. That miserable dog, for instance, that trotted at Christy's heels. A lot of the man's acts were truly Christian, yet he despised, derided the Padre's formal religion. Perhaps Christy was right. Virtue was not to be organised.

. . . . .

Doc was talking to the "reos" in his platoon.

"If any of you jokers don't think you can take it, you'd better tell me now, and I'll send you to the M.O."

There was a low murmur of protest among them. Doc looked them over contemptuously. He detested inexperience. He despised people who needed help.

"Keep your eyes on me. If I go flat, you go flat; if I start shooting, you start shooting. When the shit starts flying, there's too much noise for orders to be heard. You've got to know what you're up to, you've got to act on a signal—and act bloody lively. Or you may be dead."

The platoon was going to be his. No blow-in of an officer. *His.* And no reo was going to mess things up, after he and Corpus had been in on this stink from the word *go.*

He felt he would like to tell them exactly what they were going into, and watch their faces. But they had all guessed that action lay just ahead, so daily he was giving them the scornful edge of his tongue. Before, he had merely enforced the orders of the platoon officer, a little off-handedly, finding a cruel diversion in destroying any resistance, for he loved a clash of wills. This time, if anything went wrong, if the men played up, there was no officer to whom he could say: "You're the officer, go and do a bit of your own dirty work. I couldn't care less." If they wanted to survive with him they would have to act like soldiers.

He bared his white teeth at them in a disdainful smile.

"Personally, I'd rather take a troop of girl guides into action."

"There'd be no virgins by the time you'd finished with them," someone murmured.

. . . . .

Dearest Freda, wrote Kirk,

I have sent you some personal things of Steve Rogers to give his wife. Since you will go to see her, it might be better if you were to take them along. I know you will do your best to help her. I have already written to her myself.

He laid down his pen. What words, he wondered, did he use on these errands of commiseration to wives, mothers, or girls who had lost their boys? The same ones, over and over? For Freda, a Numerella girl, what did it feel like to know that a certain familiar figure was never to be seen again in Numerella? Did her conscience ever make an unspoken speech, like: "My husband has led your man to his death and I come to comfort you?"

A fear, poignant, half-conceded, like a flicker on a far, dark horizon, he disowned and obliterated, by taking up the pen and writing savagely, defiantly:

Ted and I had a day together recently. What a magnificent chunk he has grown into! I know how proud you must be of him—none of your pride is misplaced, none of our pride. I must confess to being a bit tongue-tied. He is so strong and fearless and self-sufficient, well able to handle the world on his own, thank you very much, that I had to hastily revise my manner, see myself as more of a brother, or, if you like, a comrade in arms . . .

The head of Major Brand came through the hessian curtain that screened the Colonel's dug-out.

"Sorry, Vic. There's a signal from Brigade."

The Colonel laid down his pen again, and rose.

The date on the half-written letter was September the third, 1942.

40

COMPANY Commanders came into Battalion for a final conference. They sped back in their vehicles to their companies, and summoned them to gather around.

Sitting above them on the humpy roof of his *doover*, Pascoe looked at their expectant and upturned faces. They had become a part of his life and would possibly be a part of his death, and he of theirs. He gazed at those faces intently, as if they held some message. Which? And why?

"All right, you jokers," called Company Sergeant-Major Watson, "we've got news for you, so be quiet."

Pascoe began to speak, slowly and clearly:

"The answer to the question you've all been asking is—dawn tomorrow."

There was a discontented murmur among them. The desert soldier hates a dawn attack, with the sun coming up to find you out on the flat desert like a fly on a wall, with tanks and guns on the ridges waiting to swat you off, and the planes straffing above like great sputtering hawks, feeling as big as a house, as helpless as an insect pinned to a board. No time to dig in before the light came. It meant bayonet charges and being pinned down . . .

Pasco waited for the murmur to die down.

"We are to advance to a certain position and hold it for twelve hours—then withdraw——"

"In an orderly fashion," mocked somebody.

"As the funny man said, in an orderly fashion. We have a sand-table and I'll show you the position on it, and describe the nature of our objective after. There is going to be a lot of opposition. They're waiting for us. Do you get that? This is no surprise attack. They're waiting for us."

And how! thought Doc.

"Now this," proceeded Pascoe, giving them a hard, direct look, "is to be a killing party. No prisoners. Understood? The old hands have probably told you that when a German surrenders it's usually a dodge to lure you above ground and mow you down. That's what happened last time. You'll find a lot of tanks out there. You've had plenty of training in how to deal with them. We're carrying sticky bombs in with us. You all know they're effective on certain parts of a tank. Don't waste them. Don't waste small-arms fire on tanks. We'll have a few tanks and armoured cars of our own. Not as many as they will. The anti-tank platoon will try and get their guns up as far as possible. Don't bet on it. We're out-numbered and the Hun will soon get wise to it, so the first impact is vital. Hit them hard and without mercy from the word *go*. I repeat, this is a killing party. No prisoners——"

"What about the rules of warfare?" somebody asked.

Pascoe at once replied:

"Fog the rules of warfare. There's only one for you to remember: destroy the enemy. Now, break off and come over to the sand-table and you'll see the kind of ground we have to attack over. Get a picture of it in your mind and of how to best make use of it."

He leapt down from the roof of the *doover* and led them over twenty yards to the sand-table, where a corporal from the Intelligence Section waited. There, they spent an hour. Officers and N.C.O.s stayed behind after the men were dismissed; finally only platoon commanders: Lieutenants Carson and Seeley and Sergeant Doc Home.

"Took it quietly, didn't they?" observed Carson.

"What other way is there?" asked Pascoe. "The army doesn't accept resignations."

• • • • •

"What'll you do," Ryman was asking Doc, "if they commission you after this stink?"

"Tell 'em to shove it. I see too bloody much of Stainforth and Orford and that mob as it is. Don't worry, they won't commission me. I'm not snotty enough, and anyway, sergeant's the best rank in the army. Sergeants win wars."

"What about privates?"

"They do what they're bloody well ordered, and I'm ordering you to shut up."

A little later Doc joined Christy in his *doover*. The dog had gone back to Battalion in the ration truck. Christy was writing.

"Well," he asked dryly, "how are your men?"

Doc grunted. "All right. Busy writing home like you."

"I'm not."

"Oh, more of that poetry stuff?"

"Perhaps. Verse, more likely."

"What's the difference?"

"A heart, a soul, a world."

"You're molo. Night before you go into action, and you squat in your *doover* writing poetry."

"Why aren't you writing home?" Christy asked him.

"Me? Who the hell should *I* write to?"

"Write to Juliet."

"Christ!" Doc chuckled. "A man ought. 'Juliet, care of the Mareka, Cairo.' "

He continued chuckling, shaking his head, and showing his teeth. "Christ what a lovely old rort!"

"Private Watford back?" asked Christy.

"Yair. Why?"

"He's a bit worried."

"Is that why he went to see the Roman Catholic Padre?"

"Yes."

"Reckon he might ringtail?"

"Any one of us might."

Doc rose. "I'll go and see him."

"Leave him alone. You'll do him no good. Leave it to me."

"O.K. I'm going back to my *doover*. Good night."

A few minutes later Christy came above ground and stood for a few moments looking up at the night sky, a dark, glowing sky where the moon rode among the galaxies. He felt his way along the edge of the communication trench until he was above Watford's *doover*. He was about to call when a pale shaft of moonlight revealed a boot and a leg in a curious position. He leaned lower and peered. There was no sound from the *doover*, but its occupant was praying.

Christy left silently.

Back at his own *doover* Pascoe was waiting.

"Hallo, Corpus. I just called to wish you good luck."

Christy nodded but did not speak.

Pascoe turned and looked Hunwards, out over the silent, sleeping desert.

"It won't be long now. They're out there waiting for us. They're waiting."

41

At three a.m. Pascoe came out of his *doover* wearing a greatcoat over which his webbing was loosely slung, a tin hat on his head. In the pale gloom outside he met the Company Sergeant-Major.

It was deathly cold. The stars were veiled behind high clouds whose shadows raced blackly across the face of a white moon. There was no sound on all the earth.

Pascoe shivered.

"Nice day for a massacre," the C.S.M. observed.

Pascoe grunted.

"Wake 'em up," he said. As if any of them would be sleeping!

. . . . .

Kirk had brought his H.Q. forward and installed himself in a command post, with lines running out to his companies. With him were Brand, Stainforth, a signaller, and a runner. They reclined quietly against the walls of the post. Kirk smoked.

His sense of foreboding would not leave him. He was only outwardly calm. This was not like other actions. He felt as though he were hurling his battalion into a bottomless pool. Something in him cried out against what was about to happen. Last night he had decided that it would have been better to put him in command of some other battalion than the one from Numerella. In battle, a commander wasn't supposed to feel for his men. Oh, God! he thought, if you *are*, let them off lightly——

The buzzer sounded and he lifted the handset of the telephone. The companies had begun to report themselves in position.

. . . . .

Christy stared at the single line he had been able to write:

Tomorrow, reality confronts us like a screaming face

Not very good, he decided. He rose suddenly and threw the pad aside. What did it matter? It was nearly first light. He had better compose himself for possible death. How did one do it? There was a conceit which said I shall go nobly, able, for the last time, to esteem myself. In all honesty, I can make no provision for afterwards: I have doubted the existence of a Maker too often, and too bitterly. Was there perhaps some shade, some dimension where the misspent life could be ruminated on? That would be fun. Might there be trees and water and laughing girls! Or broad gold pavements and ethereal cadences, in illimitable space? He doubted whether he would enjoy that.

Coming along the communication trench, Doc was telling himself that if he got knocked off this time round, he would die with the thought of that Cairo leave in his head; if he didn't, then it was back to Cairo and Juliet, and he was going to beat her, listen to her squeal with the joy of pain, until whatever it was hungering inside him was liberated.

He felt one moment of terror at the thought of being wounded irreparably in his genitals. If that happened he would want to die. If he didn't die, he would finish himself off at the first opportunity.

He entered the gun-pit where several of his platoon lay in silence against the sides.

"Right-o, you jokers. We've got an appointment with Rommel."

. . . . .

Soon all the company were out there in the darkness, the platoon commanders going murmurously among them calling a roll which would never be the same again. Quietly, as if at some devout ritual, they reported their men as all present.

Pascoe turned his face to the stars in the western sky.

"Forward," he said, and led his company to its rendezvous.

42

In the same instant as the first greying came in the eastern sky, Kirk heard the artillery open up. Above their heads, the shells flew through space, endlessly whinningly, invisibly. In the far distance, the drumfire of their explosions. Now the men would be moving forward, strung out in a thin line, trying to act like a brigade, rifles at the port, faces advancing to the enemy. He heard a drone in the sky between the noise of the shells. An enemy spotter-plane, he thought. Soon the Fifty-Fifth would strike the German artillery.

He had seen them lining up in the darkness, just forward of his command-post, looking for their marks, getting their bearings, voices queerly muted in the minutes before the air was ripped apart by the racket of guns. He had gone down the whole line calmly saying: "Good luck," and being answered mostly by an indistinguishable murmur, or nothing at all. When he had spoken to Doc Home's platoon Doc had grunted:

"We'll need it."

Don Company would have the greatest task in reaching its

objective. There was practically no cover in their line of advance. The other companies had the side of the ridge and a lot of undulating desert.

The phone buzzed again and Brand answered it. He turned to Kirk and looked at him wryly.

"They're racing," he said.

. . . . .

This is certitude! To kill or be killed—as simple as that. Pascoe exulted. He glanced to left and right of him. The men of his company strode in a long, sparse line beneath the shrilling of the shell-fire. Their figures were still dim in the grey first light and he could not yet tell one from the other.

From the ridges bulking on their left came a sudden burst of small-arms fire, the echoes lashing across the desert. A and C Companies on the southern side of the ridge and B Company on the northern had made contact with the enemy. The bursts increased and then the ridge itself was shaken and darkened by shell-fire. The greyness of the dawn was stained by boiling smoke. The Germans had found the range of the other companies swiftly, sooner than Pascoe would have thought possible. When was Don Company's turn coming? It would be worse for them down on the flat.

. . . . .

Reports came into Kirk's command-post like a torrent. A Company three hundred yards from objective and pinned down by heavy shelling from the enemy. Casualties heavy. C Company also under shell-fire. Company commander killed.

"Collinson's gone," he told Brand, who looked up, startled. Collinson had been his peace-time partner.

Kirk had a signaller at the tank rendezvous. Any time now he would get a call telling him that the "Jock" column had arrived. They would wait there until such time as any German tank activity was reported.

A mist of acrid fumes came creeping round the command-post. Through the filaments of smoke a silent procession was passing: stretcher-bearers bringing back wounded.

"Go out and get the names of some of those wounded," he told the runner, who rose and ran into the smoke.

It was wrong, Kirk told himself. He would know soon enough who and what his casualties were. But it had always been the same: he had to know at once.

"C Company line dead," the signaller said suddenly.

"Get busy," Kirk told him without looking round.

The signaller grabbed his haversack and disappeared into the reverberating fog round the command-post.

The R.S.M. called in another signaller from the gunpost alongside. The Colonel crawled up on to the observation platform above the revetment. From here he could see straight ahead in the direction of the advance, along the ridge where A, B, and C Companies were now under heavy shell-fire. He raised his glasses to his eyes and focused them on the distance, but between him and his companies was an ocean of heavy smoke. He slithered back down and asked the man at the phone.

"Anything from the tank rendezvous yet?"

The man shook his head.

"They should be there! Raise them."

The man obeyed and a few second later silently handed Kirk the handset.

"Where is that 'Jock' column?"

At the other end an anonymous voice answered:

"There's no sign of them, sir."

Kirk replaced the handset and turned savagely to Brand.

"That bloody 'Jock' column's gone A.W.L. If the Hun decides to feel us out with a few tanks or armoured cars before the column arrives, I'm going to lose a couple of companies. Get Brigade."

• • • • •

Pascoe walked a little behind the line of his company so that he could see them the better. They advanced calmly, almost casually, some of the inexperienced glancing occasionally towards the shell-harried ridge, wondering perhaps if they were in range of any of that sharp, singing shrapnel. Every few minutes Pascoe encouraged them:

"Keep going!"

Doc was watching Private Watford hawkishly. The boy's face was glossed with the sweat of terror. He walked forward mechanically, staring steadfastly ahead, his eyes fixed on some distant point in the heavens.

What does he see there, wondered Christy. A vision of the God he believes will preserve him, perhaps to the exclusion of all others?

No fogging shell-fire on Don Company yet, Doc thought. It was too good to be true. He ran round behind his platoon and along to Pascoe.

"This place is mined!" he shouted through the thunder of shell-fire. "I'll put money on it."

"Have you told your blokes to watch for fresh-dug ground?"

"What do you bloody well think I told them? The Three Bears?"

Pascoe grinned. "I don't like this set-up any more than you! Personally, I think we're all doomed!"

"Wonderful foggin' morale-builder, aren't you?" screamed Doc, and Pascoe threw his face right up at the heavens and laughed like a maniac.

Doc ran back along the line to his platoon, giving a man who lagged behind a savage kick in the stern on his way past. Why couldn't they all be like old Corpus, loping along there as though he were out for a stroll? If Corpus ever decided to crack the whole platoon would go west.

Two Very lights soared skyward on their left.

"Look!" he yelled to Christy. "A and C Companies home and hosed!"

"Yair—they're getting nicely hosed!"

. . . . .

Back at the command-post, Stainforth, his glasses trained along the southern slope of the ridge, also saw the Very lights, and came down from the platform into the pit.

"A and C Companies at objectives, sir. No signal for tank activity yet."

"Thank God," said Kirk. "The 'Jock' column's lost."

"Lost, sir?" asked the Adjutant politely.

"Yes, lost!" the Colonel told him scathingly. "L-O-S-T. Unseen. Not to be found."

"What do you think's happened?"

"Who knows? Bombed. Struck a minefield. The Brigadier is obligingly making inquiries."

His dread had materialised. This was it. He had known all along that some major factor would fail. He had never liked this plan. There was something wrong, not quite realised, only sensed. It was too clever. Too much psychology involved; too much dependence on human reaction.

The line to the rear observation-post buzzed and the signaller picked up the handset. "Thanks," he said, and replaced it.

"Stukas bombing the dummy tanks in our rear, sir."

"As soon as they think they're destroyed, or as soon as they wake up they're dummies, that's when the fun will start," Kirk told the others. "They won't do much to the companies on the ridge, but as for poor old Don . . ."

At that moment the Don Company line buzzed and the Colonel picked up the handset himself.

"That you, chief?"

"Yes, Roy. Go ahead."

"We've just struck the first enemy opposition. We're under heavy small-arms and Spandau fire—wait! That was a bloody mortar——"

"Yes, I heard it. Go forward lizard-fashion. I'll get arty on to the opposition. Is your left flank still hugging the base of the ridge?"

"My bloody oath! I've just been along there. It's a shambles. Bodies everywhere. Get arty as close to us as you can. Never mind safety margins. We suspect mines."

"Can do. What are your losses?"

"Three dead. Cameron, Evans, and Hearst. Christy has a lovely hole in the brim of his helmet."

"He would. Good luck. Mind the arty."

"So long, master," sang Pascoe jauntily, and the line went dead.

. . . . .

The first of the Spandau fire struck Don Company at extreme range. Three men flung up their arms, quivering and taut, as though gripped by some sudden ecstasy—then fell like sacks and were dead. A second later the sound of the fire chased the bullets home.

Pascoe flung his arms out rigid, then lowered them with the hands pointed to the ground, and the Company went to earth. Something glowed and crackled in front of Christy's face, and the next second his head quaked and resounded, as though it had somehow got inside some great, pealing bell. He sank to his knees, hand groping for his face.

"Oh, God!" screamed Watford. "Corpus's been hit!"

The cry was echoed down the line. Christy felt the panic travel like an electric wave. He got to his feet and shouted:

"I'm all right! I'm O.K.! LOOK!"

Her performed a staggering little dance, then went down again as bullets howled by. He found himself next to Doc who asked:

"Where do you think you are? The bloody Tiv?"

"Got an Aspro?" inquired Christy.

"This is bloody rich," C.S.M. Watkins was saying to Pascoe. "This is the heaviest small-arms fire I've ever seen. And they haven't even got our proper range yet."

"Just wait till the tanks get busy," said Pascoe. "We've got to get off these stones and into some sand before that happens."

Suddenly the deep notes of the mortars were right among them. The earth was flung upward by a dozen invisible shovels and in between the resonant notes of the mortars came the wailing of men. The bent forms of stretcher-bearers hurried through the smoke, tracing the cries of the wounded. Pascoe put his mouth to Watkin's ear:

"They've got a mortar well out in front of their positions." He turned to the runner. "Doc Home, Corpus Christy, and two others. Quick!"

The runner crawled off to the left. He returned in a few minutes with four slithering forms.

"That mortar," said Pascoe. "Get it."

"What about our arty?"

"That's a risk you'll have to take. Most of the arty's on their main positions. I place their range at over a thousand. That mortar's close—five or six hundred. Get it," he repeated.

Doc turned to the three other men:

"You heard. We've got to do that mortar over. Come on!"

He rose, and broke into a crouching run, and the others followed suit. Once clear of the concealment of the smoke and dust, he went down on his stomach again.

"It's a big 'un," he told Christy.

"Yair, probably protected by a Spandau too. They usually are."

"Remember how we did that mortar crew at Tobruk?"

"Yair. A bloke on the flank with a Bren to engage the Spandau, the others crawling in and rushing them with grenades. Standard practice."

"Here, you!" Doc called to the man with the Bren. The man came nearer. "Go out about three hundred yards and open fire on the bastards."

"I can't even see them."

"You can get their direction roughly. You'll soon know when you've got their range. They'll send a few back at you. Try it on two fifty to start. Go on!"

As the Bren-gunner was moving off, Doc told him:

"And don't try for no V.C.s. Keep flat and just draw their fire."

"Don't worry. The only V.C. I want is the Victorian coast."

Five minutes later they heard his Bren open up. He fired short bursts and awaited the reply. On the third burst the Spandau fire started and the desert rattled with a duet of Spandau and Bren. Doc and Christy were listening carefully.

"It's over there, about two o'clock from us," said Doc. "Come on."

With Christy, he began to move forward. The other man lay still. Doc turned. "Come on!" he repeated. Still the man did not move. Christy crawled back. The man lay on his face. Christy turned him over. There was a hole just beneath his cheek-bone. Blood coated his chin. His eyes were half closed and white.

"He's dead," said Christy.

Doc growled disgustedly. "Get his grenades. It's the old campaigners once again."

They commenced to crawl again. After a minute or two Christy stopped and peered. A black blob had moved in the distance.

"I saw one of their square heads just then," said Christy.

They resumed their reptilian progress.

"There it is again."

"How far do you reckon?" asked Doc.

"Forty yards."

"Too far. These are four-second grenades."

"They'll spot us in a minute."

"So what? They can't mortar us at ten yards and by the time they swing the gun on us I'll have at least two grenades on the way."

"Let's get up and rush in. That way we can both get our first grenade into the mortar pit."

Doc grinned at him. "You after another foggin' medal?"

For answer, Christy drew a grenade from his pouch and pulled the pin out with his teeth. He rose, and drawing his arm far back, sent the grenade sailing in a high arc towards the heads and shoulders that suddenly materialised in front. A second later Doc did the same. The explosions were almost simultaneous. Christy's missile hit the parapet, Doc's fell right into the pit.

They followed in behind the explosions, Thompsons firing a continuous burst. In the other pit there was a scurry of forms and the flash of gun-metal as they swung the Spandau. But Spandaus are not swung as easily as Brens. Two more grenades caught the Germans, and while Christy ran up to finish off the mortar crew Doc rushed the Spandau.

A German abandoned the gun and began to run away across the stones. With slow deliberation, Doc put his Thompson on to single shot, and, raising it to his shoulder, took careful aim. He brought the German down with his first shot. Seeing him still move, Doc came up to stand over him. The German looked up at him, mouth open foolishly, eyes beseeching. Casually, Doc shot him through the head.

There was a shot from behind and Christy emerged from the mortar pit.

"That's the lot?" asked Doc.

Christy nodded.

"Let's go home to Uncle Roy."

43

"I MUST get some air," said Kirk.

He came above ground and stood on the roof of his command-post, glasses slung about his neck. In the distance he could see the Mediterranean, a lovely pane of glass with fluent patterns of white and blue. At that moment the sun finally mounted the ridges to the east and there came from the sea a soaring spasm of light.

He took one more deep breath and went below again.

More reports. A, B, and C Companies being counter-attacked. Badly out-gunned, and more Germans coming up. C Company had made a bayonet charge and retaken a position. There were wounded they couldn't get out.

"Anything from Don?" he asked the signaller.

"The line's dead, sir. I've sent someone out to have a look."

"There's shell-fire falling behind them," muttered Kirk. "It's probably been severed by shrapnel."

Another report came in from the ridge:

"They've got the anti-tank up, sir. One carrier lost."

"Thank God! They can keep the tanks away with anti-tank on that ridge."
"C reports tanks at a thousand yards, sir."
"*Where's that 'Jock' column?*"

• • • • •

Pascoe had led Don Company forward across the stones until he found soft ground, losing three more men on the way. In the sand, they dug shallow holes and Pascoe waited for the signaller, who had gone back to find the break in the line, to catch up and restore contact. Another signaller had still walked with a reel of line, paying it out behind as the Company advanced.
"Reel's nearly finished, sir," he told Pascoe.
A few minutes later, he said:
"That's it."
"Right! Connect it up to the handset and park here. I'll send back runners with any messages for Battalion. You can phone them on."
A little ahead, they dug in. The enemy were about half a mile away.

• • • • •

At midday the firing along the ridge and on the flat slackened to a few desultory bursts.
"The German's knocked off to have a think," Kirk told Brand.
"Thank God for small mercies."
"Don't speak so soon. They've had a plane up. Soon they'll know we haven't a tank to our name. What then?"
"They can hold them off the ridge, at least."
"And Don Company?"
"Surely the 'Jock' column will arrive in time to cover their withdrawal!"
"Don't bet on it, Joe," said Kirk softly.
The signaller spoke excitedly:
"Contact with Don again, sir."
The Colonel sprang to the handset.
"Roy? How are you?"
"Holed up about seven hundred yards in front of their forward positions. I've done a recce and I'm all ready to go forward."
"Well, get stuck into them immediately. They're probably re-forming for a counter-attack. Catch 'em off balance. How many men down are you?"
"Only eleven."
The Colonel restrained himself from asking the names.
"Well, attack at once. I'll direct every piece of arty on to your sector. Got it?"
"Yes. There's a hell of a gap between us and C. I'll have to send

a section out to cover it as best it can. I thought the armour was supposed to come through there to cover our withdrawal?"

The Colonel considered for a minute. Then, harshly, he said:

"There is no armour."

Pascoe's voice lost its lightness of tone. There was a pause.

"No armour?"

"Something's slipped up. It's late. Brigade's on the job."

"That's bloody lovely!"

"Roy—listen!" There was an urgent, appealing tone in the Colonel's voice. "I've got to gamble on the armour getting here soon. The Brig wants the positions opposite you taken at once. You understand?"

"Certainly, we'll take them."

Pascoe's voice was cool again now.

"That's the lot then," said the Colonel heavily.

"Righteo! I'm at the end of my line, but I'll send runners back to the phone with any messages. And, sir?"

"Yes?"

"You'd better get the ammunition truck up at once—just in case *we* do get cut off. We haven't a great deal."

"I'll send it now. Good-bye, good luck."

. . . . .

Behind the barrage, Pascoe took Don Company forward. There came the counter-barrage, and they walked through a world of yellow swirling mist where the earth threw up thunderous black geysers and the shrill metal, sundering, ran in long tongues, crying with affliction, and cutting into the bodies of men.

Out of the cruel, racketing torment of the barrage, contact with the enemy would come as a relief—if only to die at his hands. Better death than madness.

And suddenly the enemy was presented to them. Barrage and counter-barrage ceased almost simultaneously. They rose from the sand in front of the German positions as the mist cleared, and with weird, bestial cries, flung themselves through the shattered wire.

They gunned the trenches from above or leapt down into the depths with bayonets. Outnumbered, crazed by the shell-fire, the Australians carried the Germans before them down the long, deep trenches.

The Germans retreated along the communication trenches where Doc pursued them, throwing grenades among them and then leaping to finish off the wounded, his boots slithery with blood.

His leg gashed by the wire, Christy led three men to the flank of the position, where several Germans were trying to re-man a Spandau. His grenade went wide, but it sent them to earth, and then he was upon them. Thompson leaping at his hip. The other two men were bayoneting the survivors, none of whom attempted surrender, but died hard—thrashing and struggling.

When Pascoe was certain that all the Germans were dead he ordered his men to man the captured trenches. The enemy dead were dragged up and piled about the desert, like sacks of bloody meat.

Then Pascoe sent a runner back to the signaller in the rear, with a message for the Colonel. Exultantly, he set about organising his company. Half of the Germans had escaped back to rear positions, despite the swiftness and savagery of their attack. There would undoubtedly be a counter-attack.

The first of them came in the middle of the afternoon. The Germans reached the very parapets of their former trenches, wavered, then fled when the Australians came out of the trenches at them with every weapon blazing. They ran back to their positions several hundred yards behind.

Mortars began to find them. Ryman was hit in the leg just below the knee. He lay writhing in the sand, the leg entirely severed except for a thin, shiny membrane. Christy ground the steel-shod heel of his boot on the membrane and kicked the leg out of the way. Then he drew out Ryman's field dressing and tied it round the stump. The boy's face was quite white, smoothed out, the eyes strangely lucent. Christy began to call for a stretcher-bearer.

Then came shell-fire which killed several more men. Australian shell-fire answered from the ridge away on their left. Pascoe ran along the trenches, checking his ammunition. There was not much left.

"Don't fire unless you actually see them clear," he ordered. "The ammunition truck should be up soon."

The Runner came in scrambling to Pascoe.

"The ammo truck's back there with the sig, boss."

"Good! You three men get back and start carrying it up."

"*Tanks!*" said a voice.

The whole company turned to watch the end of the ridge. Five German tanks had appeared around it, in a wake of flying dust.

"Stay here," Pascoe told the three men. "It's too late. They've seen the ammo truck."

One of the tank guns burst into life, then another. Behind Don Company a great sheet of flame leapt into the air, followed by a train of rapid explosions that lasted ten minutes; ten minutes in which Pascoe gazed and assessed the chances of his Company.

. . . . .

"Don gone dead again," Kirk's signaller told him.

Kirk nodded dully. C Company had just reported the tanks.

The Brigade line buzzed.

"Yes?" Kirk did not even bother to answer the code. His voice was a tight whisper.

"The 'Jock' column should almost be at your command-post," the Brigade Major told him.

"What happened to it?"

"I'll leave it to them to tell you. Wait a minute——"

The Brigadier's voice came on the line:

"Vic? Congratulations!"

"What for?"

"They fell for it. Air Liaison reports huge tank concentrations, beginning to break up and make south—but too late! Bring your boys out at sunset."

The Colonel did not reply.

"It worked," he told Brand." They've just woken up to the trick, but it's too late. You can start giving withdrawal orders. It's not long till sunset."

He stared at the handset as if wondering what on earth it was.

. . . . .

Coming in close, the tanks had already killed six of Pascoe's men and pinned them down long enough for Germans from the rear positions to get up to within two hundred yards and occupy their reserve trenches. The parapets were all blown away, the trenches all but collapsed. Men, wounded, and whole, lay half buried in the bottom. And ceaselessly the tank shells thumped into the earth only a few inches above their heads. The trench walls behind them shook and showered sand on them. On the other side they could hear the German infantry whom they had driven from these trenches calling exultantly.

The boy Watford was down on his knees, sobbing. Nobody took any notice of him. But suddenly he rose and scrambled out of the trench, waving something white and stumbling towards the Germans.

"I surrender!" he cried. "God says to spare me!"

There came a series of hoarse laughs, there was a clatter of fire and Watford went down riddled. The laughter repeated itself.

Pascoe looked down the trench where the men lay or sat. Some were quietly bleeding. Some were dead. The uninjured looked much like the others. It was difficult to read their expressions, for their faces were cloaked with an emulsion of sand and sweat.

"Anyone else feel like surrendering?" he asked.

There was no answer.

He crawled along to where Christy lay, and collapsing next to him, said:

"We're all going to die."

"Yair," said Christy. "Right in the fashion, aren't we?"

44

"WRONG map reference, old boy."

The Colonel stared for a full minute. His first impulse was to abandon control and laugh hysterically. Then he disbelieved what he had heard.

The Colonel in charge of the "Jock" column was a tall, soft-spoken man. There was a mixture of shame and compassion in his eyes.

"Yes. The big things all come off, the difficult things, and something is thrown right out of gear because somebody was just not as careful with a thing everyone takes for granted. Somebody repeated a map reference wrongly. It's ridiculous, isn't it?"

The Colonel still stared at him. Then suddenly he found voice. A voice that shook.

"I'll have somebody broken in two for this."

"I'll help you. But what will it prove?"

The Colonel pointed along the ridge.

"There's a company of mine out there."

"What chance have we of getting them out tonight?"

"I don't know. There's been no contact for three hours. No firing for the last hour. There are German tanks out there and I think my men are out of ammunition. My other companies are coming in, but they're too exhausted to cover any withdrawal."

"Let's go and see," said the "Jock" column commander. "Do you know their exact position?"

"No. And it's nearly sundown."

. . . . .

Just before the sun set Pascoe gathered those who were left of his Company about him in the trench, and addressed them.

"They're waiting for darkness before they come over and finish us, just in case we have a few rounds left. Don't think we have a chance to get away with the darkness. They'll make the place as bright as day with flares. It's no use surrendering. You saw what happened to Watford."

They watched him intently, eyes white in their filthy faces. Doc Home, leaning forward with his teeth bared, as though even at this last moment there was some enjoyment to be taken. Christy, composed, drawn, blue eyes sad.

"I am going to lead a bayonet charge with those who want to come. If anybody doesn't want to take part in it, if he would rather wait and die later, then he can."

There was no sound among them. No one moved. Christy turned one of the corpses over and took the rifle and bayonet from beneath it. Those without rifles and bayonets went looking for them. Armed, they spread themselves along the trench and awaited Pascoe's command.

The setting sun was full in their eyes. Across the sand there came to them the exulting voices of the Germans.

This is the Moment of Truth! thought Pascoe. Oh, Truth and Power and Maximum Joy!

He went along the trench and shook hands one by one with his Company. As he reached Christy he said:

'So all our argument has come to this."

Christy smiled. He looked very old and wise.

"We now agree on everything," he said.

"I shall stay next to you," said Pascoe.

Christy nodded, and looked aside at Doc. Doc winked. At last he saw the joke in its fullness.

"Charge!" cried Pascoe, and sprang from the ruined trench.

The dying sun blinded them. They were black and gigantic against it. The noise from the German trenches ceased suddenly. Then there were different cries—cries of disbelief and admiration.

"*Wartet-einen augenblick!*"

"*Goot in Himmel—das—ist—unslaublich!*"

. . . . .

At the end of the ridge, the two Colonels, scanning with their glasses the dimming landscape, heard a two-minute tumult of gun-fire. Then there was silence once again.

IN THE RANKS OF DEATH YOU'LL FIND HIM

45

ALL night long the Colonel stood watching the withdrawal of the last of his forces from the ridge. The search for wounded went on by the light of the moon. They came first. He spoke encouragingly to those who were conscious, and some of these told him the names of men they knew to be dead.

The the very last rays of the sun, elements of the "Jock" column had returned the fire of the remaining German tanks, which withdrew for the night. The search for the wounded was thus ended quickly. The dead could wait till dawn.

The sum of casualties began to take shape. Of A, B, and C Companies there were eighty men left standing. There remained Don Company to be accounted for.

Colonel McMahon of the "Jock" column remained with Kirk all night, sharing his water-bottle which he had filled with rum.

Wisely, he did not try and persuade Kirk to sleep. From time to time Kirk sat down on an ammunition box and took a swig at the bottle. The moon came up and struck little moons on the stones of the ridge. The slow and toiling forms of stretcher-bearers bringing back wounded became stark against the glowing sky.

Once, when a line of stretchers came by and Kirk went over to talk to the wounded, McMahon heard him exclaim:

"Not *this*, Garry!"

When Kirk rejoined him, McMahon said:

"Something pretty nasty?"

"Feet blown off." McMahon made no comment. "He was one of the best athletes in Australia."

"I shan't forget this battalion," McMahon told him quietly. "I shall never forgive the imbecile that prevented me sharing this action with it."

"I'm beginning to feel sorry for him," said Kirk. "He's the one who has to live with the memory of what a moment's carelessness has done."

"Even had nothing gone wrong, it would have been a marvel to succeed."

"It was too damned clever," said the Colonel.

46

Aᴛ first light the Colonel left the ridge and returned to his old headquarters, where Brand and Stainforth were already re-organising. He parted from McMahon, who was to take out tanks and armoured cars for reconnaissance and then make contact by radio. So Kirk's first order on his return was to put a signaller on a field radio to await McMahon's report.

Around the huge dug-out that was the Regimental Aid Post, Padre Stringer passed among the dying and the dead. He went from stretcher to stretcher, his face harsh with grief, murmuring to each man as he leaned over him. *Stringer had also spent the night with the wounded.* He had, reflected Kirk, more than once risked his life to recover the body of a dead soldier. Perhaps he should put in a citation about Stringer, along with a lot of others.

Everybody was filthy, faces cruelly drawn, yellow shirts and shorts ripped and holed by the stones. Stainforth reported the remnants of the companies back in their old positions in reserve. Kirk re-entered his old dug-out, where Brand was still reviling the "Jock" column.

"Oh, by God, there's going to be a nice old court martial soon!" he cried ferociously.

Kirk echoed McMahon's words:

"What will it prove? . . . You know," he went on, "when I was a Lieutenant I marked a map wrongly. Just one moment's loss of concentration, and I had plotted arcs of fire so that one platoon would have been shooting into another's backs. It was only an exercise, fortunately, and the man who set me right was a private. But it happened."

He slumped down on to a petrol drum as his staff stared at him.

"War is itself ridiculous," he told them tiredly, "so ridiculous things happen. That's the way battles are lost and reputations ruined: some stupid detail that manages to throw a hugely conceived plan right out of commission. We've lost a company. It might have been the entire battalion. Remember what happened to the Sixty-Second just because a driver went two feet out of his way in a minefield. Every mother's son of them lost. Twenty-four inches killed a battalion."

Early sun came through the vent in the roof of the dug-out, lighting their features: the boyish ones of Stainforth, now with bloodshot eyes and pale, tightened lips, his slim form all slumped into itself. Brand, big, heavy, his large kind face plainly showing his concern for his commander. The R.S.M., slightly wounded in the arm, looking embarrassed at the unregimental state of his clothes.

The sun turned the yellow sandy walls of the dug-out to cream and struck little silver sparks on the handset of the phone, on map-cases, and on the metal of webbing equipment.

"It's going to be a lovely day," he said, and rose.

"I'd better get stuck into the paper work," muttered Stainforth. "I'll get Price-Gore."

"No!" shouted the Colonel. "Not Price-Gore today. He'll report with a shave and polished boots and a clean shirt. That today I couldn't bear."

They all laughed. To the Colonel, their laughter sounded incredibly strange. Startling.

Stringer came into the dug-out, and seeing the Colonel uttered the one word: "Sir." Yet to them all it seemed to contain a word of meaning, grief, and anger, and perplexity.

"Peter," said Kirk, "what would we do without you?"

"I wish to God," Stringer replied sadly, "that I had never had to do what I have been doing." He shook his head resentfully. "All those fine, good boys . . ."

"That was rough on Garry Lane," the Colonel said.

"He is dead," the Padre told them. "He just threw in the sponge."

"Best quarter-miler I ever saw," growled the R.S.M.

The phone buzzed and Stainforth answered. He offered the handset to the Colonel.

"Brigade, sir."

Kirk took it and responded.

"Vic?"

"Yes, sir."

"Vic!" The Brigadier's voice trailed off. After a few seconds it began again. "To have to tell you this just after the magnificent thing you've done——"

The world went. There was only Victor Kirk and a voice.

"Ted?" he heard himself say.

". . . yes."

"Dead?"

"I'm afraid so. If I could only tell you how sorry I am——"

"Never mind, sir. How?"

"A stray burst. It was so damned unfair!" The voice was passionate, the voice of a man who suddenly hated God.

"I have a request, sir."

"Anything, Vic!"

"I would like him buried with the Numerella men."

"Of course! I'll have the—I'll bring him over myself."

"Thank you, sir. Can I hang up?"

"Good-bye, Vic."

He turned, and there was the world again, the stricken faces of his staff. Not for a moment could he bear their pity!

So he made hard his face and of his heart a citadel.